I0657177

William Henderson

Afloat with the Flag

William Henderson

Afloat with the Flag

ISBN/EAN: 9783742810809

Manufactured in Europe, USA, Canada, Australia, Japa

Cover: Foto ©Andreas Hilbeck / pixelio.de

Manufactured and distributed by brebook publishing software
(www.brebook.com)

William Henderson

Afloat with the Flag

AFLOAT WITH THE FLAG

BY

W. J. HENDERSON
AUTHOR OF "SEA YARNS FOR BOYS" ETC.

ILLUSTRATED

NEW YORK AND LONDON
HARPER & BROTHERS PUBLISHERS
1898

TO

LIEUT.-COMMANDER J. D. J. KELLEY, U. S. N.

CONTENTS

ILLUSTRATIONS

AFLOAT WITH THE FLAG

CHAPTER I

THE CAPTAIN'S SORROW

CAPTAIN HIRAM LOCKWOOD sat gazing out of the window of his unpretentious little parlor down the hot and dusty street towards the glint of blue which told where the swift tide of the North River flowed past. The brown lines of tall masts running up and down the shifting faces of the white clouds, and the yellow festoons of canvas hanging from dark yards, made a picture that might at any other time have attracted his eager attention, but just now they were lost on him, hardy old mariner that he was, and full of a real love for nautical pictures afloat or ashore. His mind was far away, and there was a mist in his eyes that would not clear up even when his daughter Minnie came and laid her gentle arms about his neck and kissed him.

1

" Father dear," she said, " you must stop worrying about Bob, or you'll be sick."

" My dear child," said the old mariner, " you can't possibly understand the way a man yearns over his own flesh and blood when it's gone astray."

" But we don't know that Bob's gone astray, do we ?"

" Well, he's left his home without his father's consent, child, and that isn't a good thing for any one to do at any time or under any circumstances."

" But I'm sure he'll come back, father."

" But when, or how ? Oh, the prodigal son is a very fine fellow when he's sighted bearing down on his old home, but he makes a heap of trouble while he's adrift."

" But, father, you must cheer up now. Here come the boys."

Three stalwart young figures were seen advancing up the street. They were young men about nineteen years of age, and all were strong, active-looking fellows, with bright eyes and sunburnt faces. They came along, keeping exact step, with a free, swinging stride and well-squared shoulders, which showed the results of sound training somewhere. And, sure enough, these young fellows had just been through four years of the most substantial mental and physical education that can be obtained in the United States, or, for the matter of that, in all the world. They were naval cadets, fresh from the United States Naval Academy at Annapolis. One of them, a dark youth, with a restless, impatient expression on his countenance, was Frank Lockwood, nephew of the captain. His father and mother had both died while he was in his early days at the Academy, and now his uncle Hiram was his guardian, and with him the boy made his home. The boy walking in the middle had a face that was full of free, careless enjoyment, as he glanced right and left at the open windows of the houses. He was George Briscomb, a classmate of Frank. The third boy was more thoughtful in appearance than the other two, though he was undoubtedly not so attractive to look upon. His name was Harold King, and he was also a classmate of Frank Lockwood. Both these boys lived in the Far West, and had decided to spend part of their furlough in New York in order to see the sights of the metropolis. At the same time they were in hopes that they would speedily receive the orders, which for some reason had been delayed, attaching them to ships for the customary two years' cruise which all naval cadets must make after completing their four years at the Academy, and before coming up for final examination for the grade of ensign. As they came up to the house, they waved their hands to the captain and his daughter, and entered with laughter and gay words.

"Where have you boys been?" asked the captain.

"Oh, off looking at the war-ships in the North River," replied Briscomb.

"You know there are a good many of the Columbian review fleet still at anchor there," said Harold, "and I think it is the duty of naval cadets to learn all they can about them."

"Exactly my sentiments," said Frank, "only they make a fellow feel sore about his own navy. Why, that young Brazilian I met out there, Lieutenant Roderigo Bennos, who showed me over the ship, simply laughed at me when I told him I thought her not so good as the *New York.* And the worst of it was he converted me before he got through talking to me. I tell you, Uncle Hiram, a vessel that carries four 9-inch guns in turrets with 18 inches of armor, and has a lot of 70-pounder Armstrongs to back them, is good enough for me. I'd like nothing better than to go to war in the *Aquidaban.*"

All three boys suddenly stopped talking, and looked furtively at the captain, who was watching them earnestly.

"You've been aboard the Brazilian battle-ship, boys?" he said, gravely.

"Frank has, sir," said Harold.

"We didn't go, because we thought we might be in his way," added George.

"And you learned nothing, of course, Frank, or you would have told me right away," said the captain.

"No, Uncle Hiram," answered Frank, "I can't say that I learned anything very definite."

"Very definite? Well, did you learn something indefinite?"

"I hardly know," replied Frank. "The young lieutenant told me that there were two or three American boys in the Brazilian navy."

"But you gave him some bearings on Bob, didn't you?" asked the captain, eagerly.

"Yes, Uncle Hiram, of course I did. All he could tell me was that he had seen a young American with reddish-brown hair and very dark eyes on board the *Tamandare* just before he sailed north."

"That must be Bob!" exclaimed the captain; "that must be my boy."

"Wait a moment," said Harold. "How old was your son Robert when he went to sea?"

"Ran away, my lad, ran away," replied the captain. "You may as well put the thing in plain English. I did all a man could do to drive all notions of the sea out of his head, and I did hope that, being brought up around ships and among sailors, he would have seen enough of the misery of the business to stay ashore. But he'd got his hands in the tar-bucket, and I suppose he had to go. Only, if he'd just have come to me and said, 'Father, I can't stand it, and I've got to go to sea,' why, I'd have sent him, though I reckon it would have made me feel pretty bad, too. But to have him just pack up his dunnage and walk off without a minute's warning, or as much as saying good-bye; well, it's pretty hard, that's what it is—pretty hard."

"Yes, sir," said Hal, "it is hard, and you have our sympathy, I can assure you."

"Thank ye, heartily," answered the captain.

"But you haven't answered my question yet," continued Harold.

"How old was he when he went away? He was just fifteen years old, my lad."

"And he's been gone two years?"

"Two years the Fourth o' July."

"Frank, did Mr. Bennos give you any idea how old the boy was that he saw on the *Tamandare?*"

"Well, he said he was a big, strapping fellow, and had a small mustache."

The captain's countenance became gloomier

than ever. "That couldn't be Bob," he said, shaking his head; "you know he was small for his age, Frank."

"But he might have grown, mightn't he?" asked George. "Sometimes fellows shoot up in a most surprising way. Why, there's Hal. He was a regular sawed-off a year and a half ago, and now look at him—five feet eleven, and still growing."

"But what makes you feel so sure that your son is in Brazil?" asked Harold.

"Why, when I made inquiries about him after he'd gone," answered the captain, "I found out that a boy answering his description had shipped on a schooner bound for the Windward Isles. When she came back, he wasn't on her, but her captain, from what I told him, was certain that he'd had my boy in his crew. And I'll go so far as to say that he told me Bob was going to make a good sailor. Well, the worst of it was that the boy ran away from the schooner down there, and I sent my schooner, the *Mary Lockwood*, down to hunt him up. We learned that he'd shipped on a schooner bound for Barbadoes. I've been a-tracking him in one way or another ever since, but I lost all trace of him three months ago in Bahia. I couldn't get anything except a sort of a rumor about him there, and it pointed towards

Rio. I suppose the end of it 'll be that I'll have to go down there myself."

" I think it would be the best thing you could do, father," said Minnie, who had just entered the room.

" I don't know, I'm sure," said the captain, relapsing into silence.

" It wouldn't take a great deal," said Frank, "to induce me to resign from the service, and ship on the *Aquidaban* in the hope of finding my cousin Bob."

" Why, Frank," exclaimed Hal, " you're talking nonsense !"

" Why couldn't we all three go to search for him ?" cried George.

CHAPTER II

GEORGE's speech was received with the sudden silence of astonishment. After a few moments had passed away, during which time all seemed to be lost in reflection, the captain raised his head and said:

"My young friend, I don't think I quite see the bearing of that last remark of yours."

"And I must admit," added King, "that I don't quite understand your idea either, Georgie. Are you quite sure you understand it yourself?"

"Now just hold on a minute," said George; "perhaps I did blurt it out a bit hastily, without quite reflecting, but all the same I know what I mean. Give me a minute or two to think it out."

They all sat and watched him gravely while he endeavored to "think it out." Finally he said:

"This is what I mean: Here are Harold and I, two classmates and close friends of Frank

Lockwood. Now his cousin runs away to sea, leaving a great sorrow behind him. What I say is that it is our first duty, as the friends of Frank Lockwood, to join with him in the search for the missing Robert."

"But, my boy," said Captain Lockwood, who was evidently much moved by George's earnestness, "aren't you going to think of your own future?"

"How do you mean, sir?"

"Why, if you're going off to hunt for my boy Bob, how about your duty as a naval cadet?"

"But I think we could get leave of absence for two or three months, sir. They don't seem to be in any hurry at Washington to attach us to any ships."

"And if we could get leave," said Harold, "what then?"

"Why, we'd sail in one of Captain Lockwood's vessels for Rio Janeiro, and begin the search there. You needn't look at me so doubtfully, Hal. I mean just what I say."

"I know you do, George, and my heart is with you in this plan, but I am trying to examine it all round, to see how we can carry it out."

"Captain Lockwood," said George, "if we can all three get leave of absence, will you furnish us with the ship?"

"That I will not," said the captain.

The boys looked at him in astonishment.

"Don't you approve of my plan?" said George.

"No, I do not," answered the captain. "And if I did, I shouldn't start you down on a sailing-craft. Why, you might take up the whole of your leave in reaching Rio. If I approved of your plan, I'd buy you tickets there and back by one of the mail-steamers. But, as I said before, I don't approve."

"Why, Uncle Hiram?" asked Frank. "Don't you think we can find Robert?"

"I don't know," said the captain. "To tell you the truth, though, I more than half believe that three such bright, smart fellows would do it."

"Then why won't you let us try?"

"Because," replied the captain, "I can't consent to seeing you three boys take a step that might get the authorities in the Navy Department down on you, and spoil your whole future. You take my advice, and don't you go to doing anything so foolish as to ask for leave of absence right at the beginning of your service. It 'll hurt you."

The three boys were silent for several minutes, and all of them looked very thoughtful. At length Harold arose, and said:

" Fellows, you want to find the captain's son for him if it can be done, don't you?"

" Yes."

" Well, will you shake hands with me that we'll all three go to South America to hunt for him, provided it can be done without asking for leave of absence?"

" Certainly."

" Then what's to prevent us from making application to the department to be attached to one of the vessels on the South Atlantic station? That 'll take us right into Rio, and, once there, we can easily get ashore and start the search."

" Hurrah!" cried George. " Hal, you have a big brain. And wasn't I stupid not to think of that?"

" This plan will not call out your disapproval, will it, captain?" said Hal.

" No, indeed, my lad," answered the captain, heartily. " I can't tell you how grateful I am to you two boys for your friendship to Frank and me. If you find my boy, the good Father of us all will surely reward you."

" Now, fellows," said Harold, " let us shake hands on it."

Just at that moment Minnie, who had left the room, returned with two long envelopes in her

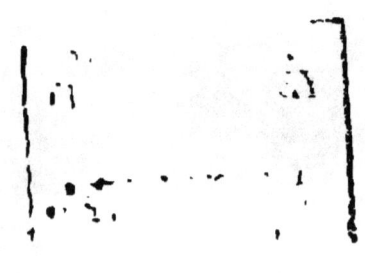

hand. "Two letters," she said; "one for Harold and one for George."

A single glance at the envelopes told the boys what to expect.

"Orders!" exclaimed George.

"It is too late for us to make application now," said Harold.

"Perhaps we sha'n't need to!" exclaimed George, tearing open his envelope. "Let us see where we are ordered to."

CHAPTER III

PREPARING TO OBEY

GEORGE tore open the envelope addressed to him, and read as follows:

BUREAU OF NAVIGATION, NAVY DEPARTMENT, }
June 20, 1893. }

Naval Cadet George Briscomb:

You will immediately report for duty to Commander Willard H. Brownson, aboard the U.S.S. *Detroit*, now at Norfolk.

FRANCIS M. RAMSAY,
Chief of Bureau of Navigation and Office of Detail.

"The *Detroit!*" exclaimed Harold.

"The *Detroit!*" cried George. "We'll be shipmates."

"Are you ordered to her too?"

"Yes, and immediately."

"That's simply too fine for anything," said Harold.

"I congratulate you two fellows," said Frank, rather sadly.

"Frank," said George, "I'm awfully sorry you're not going with us."

"So am I," added Harold; "but you know it was not to be expected that the kings down at Washington would consider our wishes. We are in the service, and we must obey orders."

"But, boys," suddenly exclaimed Captain Lockwood, "didn't I read somewhere lately that the *Detroit* was to be ordered to the South Atlantic station?"

"Is that so?" cried George.

"Wait a moment," said Harold. "I read that, too, but I am quite sure I have read since that the order had been countermanded, and that she was to remain on the North Atlantic station."

"But even that would mean a voyage to the West Indies in the fall," said Captain Lockwood, "and down there you might get on the track of my boy."

"You may depend on one thing, sir," said Harold, earnestly; "we have made up our minds to help you look for your son, and wherever we go we'll leave no stone unturned to find him."

Captain Lockwood grasped the boy's hand and shook it heartily.

And now began a time of bustle and hurry, for the orders said "immediately," and that meant that they must be obeyed within twelve hours.

"The first thing to do is to answer, isn't it?" asked George.

"Of course," said Harold. "Hurry up, too; we've lots to do."

Some regulation navy paper and two dignified white envelopes were procured, and then the two boys sat down and wrote letters like this:

NEW YORK, *June* 21, 1893.

SIR,—I have the honor to acknowledge the receipt of the Bureau's order of the 20th for duty aboard the U.S.S. *Detroit*, and will proceed in obedience thereto.

I am, very respectfully, your obedient servant,

HAROLD KING,

Naval Cadet, U.S.N.

To Commodore Francis M. Ramsay, U.S.N., Chief of the Bureau of Navigation and Office of Detail.

"There!" said Harold, as he sealed his up; "now I'll go right out and post these, and at the same time hunt up a railway guide, and see at what time we can start for Norfolk."

"And while you're gone," responded George, "I'll be getting our things together."

"I'll help you, if you'll let me," said Minnie.

"It won't take long," answered Harold, laughing, as he went out.

"A sailor don't need much dunnage," Captain Lockwood said.

Frank stood at the window, drumming on a pane of glass with impatient fingers.

"Come, Frank," said George, "be a good fellow and help me to pack up."

"All right," he answered; "but you mustn't blame me for feeling sore because I'm not going with you."

"I don't; but just think, you may be ordered to the *New York* when she goes into service."

"Not much chance of that. Those gilt-edged berths are only for the elect."

A few moments later Harold came briskly in, with a fine color in his cheeks and a bright light in his eyes. "It's all right," he said; "we can leave at ten o'clock to-night, and be there early in the morning. I've got an expressman who has agreed to take our trunks down at that outrageous hour. But I wonder what's the matter with me—I feel so light?"

"I'll tell you," said Captain Lockwood: "You're hollow. You haven't had your dinner."

"But it's all ready now," said Minnie.

Captain Lockwood led the way to the dining-room, and for a few minutes they were all silent

2

as they attacked the smoking dishes which had
been prepared under Minnie's supervision.

"There!" said George, as he laid down his
napkin at the close of the meal; "trunks packed
and ready to go; boys packed, too, and department informed. I guess there's nothing more
to do."

"Yes," said Harold, "there's one thing more.
We must go and telegraph to our mothers."

"That's so!" cried George, jumping up. "Come
on, Hal; let's go and do that right away."

And George rushed out, followed with less
haste by his more deliberate classmate.

CHAPTER IV

"How delighted my mother will be when she gets this!" exclaimed George, as he hastily scribbled his despatch.

"I don't know that my mother will be so remarkably glad," said Harold.

"Why not?"

"Because I think she had a little hope that I would be kept ashore long enough for her to make a trip to the East and spend a week or two with me."

"Well," said George, speaking slowly and rather thoughtfully, "I don't know but my mother would have liked pretty well to see me before I got under way for blue water; but who knows? We may be tied up in a navy-yard for two or three months, and so our mothers may manage to come and see us, after all."

"That's so, Geordie," said Hal, speaking affectionately. "You have a happy way of seeing things at their best."

"Oh, I suppose that's because I don't like to look at them the other way."

"We must make a move," said Harold; "we have none too much time to spare."

As the boys passed out of the telegraph-office they noticed a man in the dress of a United States sailor standing on the sidewalk, staring through the window. The man turned, and, pulling off his cap, scratched his head. Then he said:

"Beggin' yer pardon, gentlemen, could ye tell me wot the time are?"

"Yes, my lad," said Harold, pleasantly; "it's half-past eight. Can't you see the clock in the telegraph-office?"

"Oh, sure! I sees the clock all right, but wot I doesn't see are the time. Them there new-fangled figurations on the frontispiece o' a clock ain't no good fur to steer by at all. I reckon I'd run foul o' midnight if I was a-huntin' fur the fust dog-watch by one o' them figurated clocks."

Harold and George smiled, and were about to pass on, when the man turned again and spoke:

"Beggin' yer pardon the second time, I'd like to know wot are the nearest way to the Penn-sylvany Railroad ferry. I reckon my dunnage are down there, an' it are my opinion that I ought to be there too."

Harold looked at the embroidered mark on the man's sleeve, and saw that he was rated a cockswain. "Cocks'n," he said, "you just walk down to the end of the block, and take a car going to your left, and it'll take you within a block of the ferry."

"Thank ye kindly, sir," said the man. "Cocks'n I are, an' cocks'n I'm likely to be. An' my name are Peter Morris, at your sarvice, sir. An' so good-night."

With that the sailor started at a rapid though lumbering gait in the direction indicated.

"I always feel sorry for a sailor wandering about a great city at night," said Harold.

"Why?" asked George.

"Because he's sure to come to grief."

"I don't see why."

"It's the nature of the species. Why, look! Our friend the cockswain is in trouble now."

George's eyes followed the direction in which Harold's finger was pointing, and saw that the cockswain had got into an altercation with three men not more than half a block away. The warfare of words lasted only a few seconds, and then one of the three men aimed a blow at the sailor, who instantly began to lay about him most vigorously.

"Come on!" cried George, breaking into a run, "or he'll be murdered."

"We may miss our train, and not get to Norfolk in time," exclaimed Harold; "but we mustn't stand by and see a Jacky beaten this way."

The two boys went down the street at a swinging trot, taking care not to wind themselves, and to husband their strength for the encounter which they felt must now take place.

"Stop that!" cried Harold, as he and George came up to the struggling men.

A fierce reply was uttered by one of the cockswain's assailants, who at once made a desperate lunge with his right fist at Harold. The boy sprang aside, and countered on the ruffian's jaw with unpleasant force.

"That's it!" cried Peter Morris, the cockswain; "let him have it broadside fur broadside. I kin sink this 'ere slob, if you gentlemen 'll ram the others."

Harold and George engaged the attention of the other two assailants, and for a few minutes the battle waged hotly. Both boys had their blood up, and they were making good use of scientific boxing learned at Annapolis. The roughs who had assaulted the sailor were beginning to show signs of distress, and the cockswain cried exultingly:

"Strike yer colors, ye slobs! Don't ye know when you're licked?"

" ' WHY, LOOK ! . . . THE COCKSWAIN IS IN TROUBLE NOW.' "

"Hit 'im with yer brass knuckle, Jimmy!" cried one of the fellows.

"No, you don't!" exclaimed George, driving his right fist into the man's face.

"Cops!" cried another of the men.

At that very moment, when victory seemed to be certain for our young friends, two policemen came running up, and before the boys and the sailor could recover from their amazement one of the roughs had made a complaint against them, and they found themselves under arrest and marched off to the police-station.

"Waal," exclaimed Peter Morris, "as my mother used to say when she were a-mashin' pertaters, 'This are simply crushin'!'"

At the station one of the roughs told a remarkable story of how the sailor had tried to snatch his watch, and how the two young men had come up and joined in the assault on them when they tried to defend themselves. As for Peter, he was so astounded that he told a miserably bungling story of the real act—an attempt to snatch his pocket-book, which he had incautiously exposed—and the sergeant on duty said the seaman was drunk, and ordered all three of them to be locked up for the night on a general charge of assault and battery.

"But we shall miss our ship!" exclaimed Harold.

"Miss your ship! You never saw a ship," said the sergeant, contemptuously. "Take them down and lock them in."

CHAPTER V

IN AND OUT OF THE SERVICE

" I PROTEST against this as an outrage!" cried George.

"No back talk!" exclaimed the sergeant.

"One moment, please," said Harold, politely. "We are naval cadets, and are under orders to leave New York to-night to join our ship, the *Detroit*, to-morrow."

"W'y, that are my case, too," said Peter. "I ought to ha' gone this mornin', but I got lost somehow from the crowd that went from the *Vermont*."

" That is a likely story!" said the sergeant.

" If you'll send for Captain Hiram Lockwood, he'll tell you it's true," said Hal.

"Captain Lockwood? Do you know him?" asked the sergeant.

" We are visiting at his house."

The sergeant thought a moment, and, as the house was only a block away, sent an officer there. He returned in a few minutes with the captain and Frank, who promptly confirmed the story of the boys.

"Well, Captain Lockwood, I know you, and this looks quite straight now, but I'd like to see these young gentlemen's orders."

Fortunately, the boys had the orders in their pockets. They were now released, together with the cockswain.

"By the great hook block!" exclaimed the captain, "you've no time to spare. We'd better take a carriage."

"Cocks'n, you go with us," said Hal.

A coach was procured, and with the captain and the three boys inside and Peter on the box with the driver it went rattling away.

"We'll be lucky if we're not left," said George.

"We'll make it if we don't break down," said the captain. "Meantime, boys, don't worry yourselves about hunting for Bob. Only if you get the chance, do what you can."

"That's all very fine," said Frank Lockwood to himself; "but their chances of searching for Bob are done. I have no orders, and I'll not sit still in idleness. I am the one who will find my cousin."

Clang, clang! went the bell in the ferry-house as the carriage drove up. The boys bounded out and rushed to the ticket-office.

" Hold the boat for ten seconds!" cried Captain Lockwood. And, strange to say, it was done, so that the boys and Peter jumped aboard just as it moved out.

Bright and early the next day, attired in service uniform with swords and white gloves, the two cadets went off in the Norfolk navy-yard launch to the *Detroit*, which was lying off shore.

" Isn't she a little beauty !" exclaimed George, gazing with hungry eyes on the cruiser now to be his home.

" She is that," answered Harold, heartily.

Their enthusiasm was well deserved, for the *Detroit* is as neat a craft as ever filled a sailor's eye. She measures 257 feet long, 37 feet in beam, and 14 feet 6 inches in draught. She has two masts, fore and aft, schooner rigged, with the usual signal-yard at the foremasthead. She has a top-gallant forecastle and poop, and two smokestacks. Her armament consists of two 6-inch breech-loading rifles — one mounted on the poop, and the other on the forecastle, and eight 4-inch rapid-fire guns on the poop and main decks. She has the usual secondary battery of Hotchkiss rapid-fire guns. Of course she is painted white. All the ships of our new navy are white, so that the term " white squadron," originally used to designate the first squadron of four — *Chicago, Atlanta, Boston,* and *York-town*—is now out of date.

"I wonder what sort of a fellow the first lieutenant is?" said George.

The executive officer of a ship, who is second in command, is always called the "first lieutenant," no matter what his rank may be, just as the commanding officer, though he may be only a lieutenant-commander, is always called "captain."

"It can't make any difference to us," said Harold; "we've got to obey him anyhow."

"Yes, but he can make it mighty unpleasant for us."

"Not if we attend to our duties."

The launch ran alongside the starboard accommodation-ladder, and Harold led the way up. On reaching the deck both boys faced aft and lifted their caps. This salute to the flag which floats at the taffrail is never omitted. The officer of the deck approached and lifted his cap.

"Come on board, sir, to report for duty," said Harold, standing attention.

"Ah, Mr. King and Mr. Briscomb, I suppose," replied the officer, pleasantly. "Orderly." A marine in dress uniform and white gloves was standing under the break of the poop in front of the door leading to the captain's cabin. He came forward and touched his cap. "Inform the captain that Cadets King and Briscomb have come aboard."

The marine saluted and went into the cabin. In a few moments he returned and said to the officer of the deck :

"The captain says, sir, to please send the gentlemen in." The boys followed the orderly, who led them to the after-cabin. There they found themselves before Commander Brownson, a man whose grizzled hair and bronzed face bore the marks of long and honorable service under the flag affectionately called " Old Glory."

" We have the honor to report for duty according to orders, sir." said Harold, as he and George handed to their commanding officer the letters received from Washington the night before.

" I see you have lost no time, young gentlemen," said Commander Brownson, glancing at the postmarks on the envelopes. " I trust you will always be as prompt and accurate in obeying orders."

" We shall try to be, sir," said Harold.

Something in the quiet modesty of the boy's manner impressed the commander, and he smiled pleasantly as he wrote his name across the papers and said :

" Take your orders to the officer of the deck."

And now began a long, arduous summer of routine and drill, the monotony of which was broken only by the pranks of the older cadets. They were bent on making the introduction of our two young friends into the service as lively as possible, and for weeks the boys were subjected to a series of petty annoyances such as they had not known since they were in the fourth class at the Academy. They bore it all very patiently, however, for their Annapolis experience had hardened them to this sort of thing. The older cadets were under the delusion that the executive officer did not have his eye on them; but he was preparing to put down the disorder with a stern hand, when an incident occurred which ended it suddenly and decisively.

George and Harold had just received a letter from Frank Lockwood, and it made them thoughtful. " I suppose you fellows have heard of the breaking out of a revolution in Brazil," he said. " I can't stand this inactivity any longer, so I have resigned from the service, and am going to Rio Janeiro to hunt for Bob. I shall enlist with the insurgent Admiral Mello. I mean to try for a berth on the *Aquidaban*, and I'll bet you I shall see some fighting."

The two boys had read this just before going on deck for their watch, and they were now standing near a port on the spar-deck discussing it.

"How can he search for his cousin and be in the service of the rebels?" said George.

"Poor Frank!" sighed Harold, "always crazy for adventure. He will live to be sorry that he has left the service of our flag for that of a foreign one."

Just then the time arrived for relieving the watch, and as George turned to go aft the rammer of the gun beside which he had been standing was suddenly thrust between his legs. He made a violent effort to save himself from falling, and instead of doing so turned himself around, lost his balance, and fell through the open port into the water.

"You brute!" exclaimed Harold, to the now frightened cadet, who had been too playful. "He's a miserable swimmer."

And without pausing to take off his coat, Harold jumped into the water. Peter Morris, the cockswain, was leaning over the rail at the time of George's mishap, and he yelled at the top of his leathery lungs:

"Man overboard!"

In an instant there was a commotion on the ship as the officer of the deck sang out:

"Call away the whale-boat! Heave a buoy there!"

"It are all werry well," muttered Peter Morris through his shaggy brown beard; "but if one o' them boys can't swim werry good, two of 'em's werry likely to git drownded, 'less Peter Morris are also in the water, w'ich the same here goes."

And with that the honest fellow plunged overboard, and struck out for the spot where Harold, weighed down with his water-soaked clothing, was making a desperate struggle to keep George and himself afloat.

CHAPTER VI

"Beggin' your pardon, sir," said Peter, seizing George by the collar.

A few minutes later the three were hauled into the whale-boat, and were taken aboard the ship, where they were at once sent to the sick-bay to be attended by the surgeon. Peter did not seem to be in need of attention, but he was much concerned about George, who was almost unconscious. The efforts of the surgeon restored him, however, and then Harold turned around and held out his hand.

"Morris," he said, "I think he would have pulled me under if it hadn't been for you, and so you really saved both of us."

The cockswain pulled off his wet cap, which had stuck to his head, and shook the young officer's proffered hand.

"Bless ye, sir," he said, "it are all in the way of a day's reckonin'. An' you did me a good turn in Noo York, sir."

"Well," said Harold, "I sha'n't forget this."

3

This incident was the beginning of as warm a friendship as could possibly exist between a seaman and two junior officers, for George proved to be quite as sensible of the cockswain's gallantry as Harold. And this occurrence made the older cadets realize that they had carried their practical joking too far, and there was an end of it.

One morning the bugle seemed to sound the reveille with a new vim, and the men tumbled out of their hammocks with unwonted celerity. For several hours all was bustle and hurry on the *Detroit's* decks. In the midst of it all the two boys met their friend, Peter Morris, under the break of the forecastle.

"Peter, we're going to sea, sure," said George.

"Werry good, sir, says I. 'Cos w'y: ships is built to go to sea."

"I suppose the men are all wondering where we're bound," said Hal.

"No, sir; most on 'em knows."

"Then they know more than we do!" exclaimed George.

"A werry good deal more, sir. Some on 'em knows we're goin' to China to join the *Lancaster*. an' some knows we're goin' to England. Others knows we're goin' to Noo York, an' more knows that we're goin' to the West Injies.

Werry good, says I. But them as don't know nothin' don't make no mistakes."

And the cockswain walked away, gravely shaking his head. For some days after this all hands were busy in getting stores of various kinds aboard. Finally all this work was completed, and the *Detroit* left the wharf to lie at anchor in the stream, while she flew a square red flag at her fore-truck, signifying that she was getting her powder aboard.

At last all was ready, and to the steady haul of the steam-gear the anchor came slowly in. It was secured for sea, and before the sun peeped over the distant purple rim of the horizon the white hull of the cruiser was cleaving the green waters off Lambert Point, with the oily swell of a smooth sea brimming around her fore-foot. Harold gazed straight ahead of him, and saw the tremulous ripples aglow with the glory of sunrise, and it seemed as if the ship were carrying him straight into sailors' paradise. For many days the *Detroit* glided through an ocean of enchanted peace, but there finally came a change.

"Double-lens your eyes to-night, Mr. King," said the navigator, as Harold came on deck for the first watch. "I am steering to make the South Point Light on Barbadoes to get a new departure."

"Very good, sir," replied Harold. "I'll keep a bright lookout myself, sir, and see that the men don't soldier."

"If I'm any judge of signs, we'll have a taste of weather inside of twenty-four hours."

"Yes, sir," said Harold.

The boy was too well disciplined to venture an opinion unasked in the presence of his superior, but he had noticed that the stars appeared to be veiled in moisture, and that there was a deep-chested breathing in the long swell from the southward and eastward.

"Barometer 29.80," muttered George, who was in the habit of talking to himself under his breath when he was alone; "wind S.S.E., with a force of 4. Character of clouds, stratified; percentage of clear sky, 10; thermometer, 76°; wet bulb, 68°; there."

George was making the entries in the log-book at the end of his first hour on watch. Two bells pealed in dreary discord, and the lookouts forward passed the hoarse hail of "Mast-head and starboard lights burning brightly — port light burning brightly." The running lights were sending long, flickering shafts of red and green out upon the ocean ahead of the ship, and one could see the big, shiny billows glancing along towards the bows as the ship lifted her ram over the crests. and then plunged it, with a great roaring and whitening of foam, into the black hollows.

"Where was that blessed barometer at eight bells?" muttered George. "Whew! It's coming down with a rush. We're going to get a gale of wind right in the teeth."

He went out of the chart-house, and received a volley of rain-drops, driven horizontally into his face.

"Here it comes," he said, "all a-piping out of the southeast."

For twenty-four hours it blew as it knows how to blow in the regions around the equator, and then it cleared up with amazing swiftness. The course of the cruiser was set once more, and now the men began to suspect her destination.

"If I might make so bold as to ask, sir," said Morris, who was on duty near Harold, "what are the course?"

"Southeast by east," answered Hal.

"Then this 'ere ship are bound around Cape St. Roque."

"You've been there, then."

"Bless ye, sir, I bin all over this 'ere bloomin' globe, I have, an' this 'ere wessel are a-headin' fur Brazil."

"Of course; every one knows that now."

"Wot I hears I hears, an' wot I knows I knows; but wot I hears afore the mast I doesn't allus know, sir."

"Well, Peter, we're surely bound for Rio, to help to protect American interests there. Mello's rebellion has turned out to be a serious matter, and the Navy Department is going to have in Rio Harbor one of the strongest fleets the United States has ever got together."

"W'ich the same it are werry good. 'Cos w'y: them dagos 'ain't got no respect fur our flag."

"Well, there's going to be a different tune sung now."

"W'ich are the tune o' 'Yankee Doodle.' Preehaps it 'll so happen as we'll have to take a hand in the muss."

"I hope not," said Harold. "Fighting the *Aquidaban* would be no joke. Besides, there is something else."

"An' wot might that be, sir?"

"George and I would have to fight against our friend and classmate, Frank Lockwood."

"That would be a werry bad business."

"Sail-l-l ho-o-o!" came the clear cry from the foretop.

The usual questions and answers followed, and

it was learned that a wreck lay almost ahead of the *Detroit*.

"Evidently the work of last night's gale," said Mr. Burrell.

All hands were now intensely interested, for there might be living human beings in need of assistance aboard of her. The cruiser bore down on the dismasted hulk wallowing pathetically in the long, glassy swells.

"There's a man, sir!" cried Harold, whose keen eyes had detected a hand waving from one of the cabin ports.

"Call away the second whale-boat!" cried Mr. Burrell, in short, sharp tones.

The boatswain's shrill pipe and hoarse cry of "Away, second whale-boat!" sent willing feet scurrying along the sloping deck. The cruiser's engines were stopped and reversed, and George was ordered to go with the whale-boat to bring off the wrecked crew. The boy obeyed most willingly, for it was his first experience of the kind and had all the excitement of novelty. He found some difficulty in getting the whale-boat under the lee quarter of the schooner, for such the vessel was, but finally succeeded in doing so. The man who had waved his hand from the cabin now appeared, crawling painfully along the deck.

"Are you hurt?" called George.

"My knee is sprained, sir," answered the man.

"Where are the others of your crew?"

"The Lord alone can tell that, sir. We was dismasted in the gale yesterday morning, sir, just before daylight, and I never saw a soul afterwards. All knocked overboard, sir, and drownded."

"Can you get into the boat?"

"I guess so, sir."

The man reached the boat with great difficulty and much pain.

"God bless you, sir, and the flag you're flyin'! It does my heart good to see an American cruiser. Are you goin' to Brazil?"

"Yes. Why do you ask?"

"You're needed there, sir. They're treatin' Americans shameful down there, though there's some of us in their service, too."

George's heart gave a sudden bound.

"Did you know anything about any of them?"

"I saw some of them, sir."

George rapidly described Robert Lockwood to the sailor, and asked if he had heard or seen anything of such a young man.

"Seen him? Sure enough, sir. Why, he went down there as a hand on that very schooner you've just taken me off, an' a good hand, too."

"GEORGE WAS ORDERED TO GO WITH THE WHALE-BOAT."

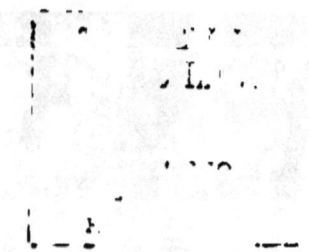

" And where is he now?"

" That's what I don't know, sir. He left us there, an' some says he's shipped with Mello, an' some says he's with Peixoto."

As soon as they reached the *Detroit*, and George had completed his duty, he ran to tell Harold the news.

" He must be down there somewhere, Hal," he said.

" It looks that way," said Hal, " and I think we have as good a chance of finding him as Frank, if not better."

" Anyhow, we can keep our word to the captain and go on with the search."

CHAPTER VII

THE troubles which had broken out in Brazil in the autumn were rapidly reaching their climax. It was a curious spectacle, upon which the entire civilized world was looking with interest. The navy of a large and powerful republic had revolted against the government, and, shut up in a few stanch cruisers, lay at anchor in front of the capital city, which it bombarded with great regularity, but little accuracy. The ostensible cause of the revolt was the veto by President Peixoto of a law making it impossible for him to be his own successor in office. The true cause was a determination to restore the monarchical government in Brazil. Week after week, month after month, the insurgent fleet continued its depredations, in spite of the belief that the rebellion must speedily collapse for the want of funds and munitions of war. Somehow these necessaries found their way into the hands of the rebel chiefs, but it was not until Admiral Mello was deposed and Admiral Da Gama placed in command that the latter's declaration in favor of monarchy revealed the true state of affairs. But President Peixoto proved himself equal to the demands of the time. Trusted agents in New York set about organizing a fleet. The merchant steamers *El Cid* and *Britannia* were purchased, and hastily transformed into cruisers. Both were supplied with torpedo tubes and effective batteries of rapid-fire guns. In addition to these, *El Cid*, rechristened *Nictheroy*, after a suburb of Rio de Janeiro, was provided with a dynamite gun—a new and untested weapon whose value in active warfare was an unknown quantity. Admiral Da Gama had once inspected dynamite guns in New York, and he had made a report on them to his government. He had a wholesome respect for the weapon. Furthermore, the agents of the Brazilian President had purchased the Ericsson submarine gun-vessel, a Yarrow torpedo-boat, and five German torpedo-boats. It was the rumor in Rio Harbor that the government fleet was to assemble in some one of the sequestered harbors along the northeastern coast of Brazil, and thence steal down upon Da Gama. Shut up in Rio Harbor, with the shore batteries behind him and the loyal fleet blocking the entrance to the bay, his position would be precarious.

But Da Gama was not disposed to wait in idleness for the decisive blow. He stole in and out of the harbor at unexpected times, so that no one could tell just where he was. With his fleet, consisting of the *Aquidaban*, commanded by the deposed Mello, the *Republica*, *Tiradentes*, *Guanabara*, *Libertade*, *Tamandare*, *Trajano*, and a few smaller vessels, he hovered like a mysterious pirate among the islands of the bay, and occasionally opened fire upon the city.

The harbor of Rio de Janeiro is justly celebrated as the most beautiful in the world. The entrance is between two bold points, 1700 yards apart. Just inside, and nearer to the western point, Fort Lage rises out of the water. On the eastern point stands Fort Santa Cruz and a fixed white light, visible six miles. On the western point are Forts San João and St. Theodosio. The harbor extends almost north and south. Outside of the eastern point of entrance, about a mile to the southeast, is Flora Point, from which runs back a spur of mountains nearly 1100 feet high. Three-quarters of a mile to the southward of Fort San João the Pao de Acucari, or Sugar Loaf, lifts its dome-like back 1270 feet above the level of the sea.

Inside the entrance the harbor widens out. On the easterly side, behind Jurujuba Point, a

little over a mile north-northeast of Fort Santa
Cruz, opens the bight of Three Fathom Bay—
a large expanse of shallow water, bordered by
San Francisco Xavier Beach on the east, and
by Carahy Beach on the north. The northern
boundary of Three Fathom Bay is a neck of
land half a mile wide, at whose outer extrem-
ities are two forts, Boa Viagem and Gravata.
Now comes another bight, forming Praia Grande
Bay, on which fronts the town of Nitheroy or
Nictheroy. To the northward of Nictheroy is
Arcia Point, a bold headland rising to a height
of 550 feet, and beyond this is a cluster of hilly
islands.

Inside the entrance on the western side is a
small bight, bordered by Urca and Botofogo
beaches, and extending to Flamingo Point, one
mile west of Fort San João. Flamingo and Frei-
ras beaches extend to the northward a mile and
two-thirds, when the city of Rio de Janeiro is
reached. Five-eighths of a mile off shore to the
southeast lies the island of Villegaignon, on
which there is a strong fort. Two hundred
yards off the point at the northeastern extrem-
ity of the city is the Isla de Cobras, on which
there is a fine dock 385 feet long. Between
these two islands is the anchorage for men-of-
war, and to the northwest of Cobras Island is

the anchorage for merchant vessels. Rat Island, on which the Custom-house stands, is 250 yards outside of Cobras Island. Enchadas Island faces the city a little over five-eighths of a mile north of the Isla de Cobras. To the northward the harbor opens out into a magnificent bay. The coast-line around Rio de Janeiro Harbor is over sixty miles in extent. There are from eight to ten fathoms of water on the bar at the entrance, while inside the depth runs from ten fathoms several miles above the city to twenty-eight half a mile north of Fort Lage.

These facts are necessary to a thorough understanding of the incidents about to be described in this story; but they give no idea of the enchanting beauty of Rio de Janeiro Harbor. Those who have ascended the Hudson River in a steamboat may conceive some faint idea of the glories of Rio Harbor by calling to mind the passage of the river between the mountains near West Point. But at Rio you come in from the open sea and behold the mountains apparently rising out of the rich blue waters. As you pass in you are close enough to see the luxuriant wealth of the tropical vegetation on the sides of the acclivities, and when you have entered the bay you are in a vast and splendid natural basin, with the dwellings and towers of the city rising proudly on your left against a background of flashing waters and olive mountain slopes.

CHAPTER VIII

UNDER A FOREIGN FLAG

WE must now go back to a time previous to the events of the last chapter. The *Aquidaban* was lying at anchor with her consorts far up the harbor off Engenha Island. The silence and luscious warmth of the tropical night were about her. Near at hand the dark hulls of the other vessels of the fleet showed black and threatening against the starlit waters. At some distance away lay the war-ships of the foreign powers represented in Rio Harbor. Great Britain, the haughty "ruler of the seas," had three cruisers there; Italy, three; Germany, two; France and Portugal, each one. "Old Glory" was not represented in the bay except by unfortunate merchant ships. These were compelled to endure all kinds of high-handed treatment by the insurgents, who asserted that they were conveying stores to the government.

No sound, except the clinking of the cables as the vessels rode to the tide, and an occasional snatch of sailor song from a wandering boat, broke the silence that surrounded the dark men-of-war. Leaning over the quarter-rail of the *Aquidaban* was a young man whom his Naval Academy friends would hardly have recognized as Frank Lockwood. The deep sunburn on his face did not hide the heavy hollows under his eyes, nor the deep lines around his mouth. Frank looked ten years older than he was on the day when Harold and George had parted from him in his uncle's house. The boy stared at the blinking lights of the distant city, and heaved a sigh that was almost a groan. A light footstep followed by a tap on the shoulder caused him to start.

"Ah, Roderigo," he said, "is it you?"

"*Si, amigo mio.* You seem not happy," said Lieutenant Roderigo Bennos.

It was the young officer who had shown the boy over the *Aquidaban* in New York Harbor.

"No, I'm not," replied Frank, shortly.

"Why are you not happy? Here we fight much—all the time—every day. That is what you say you want."

"But such fighting!" exclaimed Frank. "We lie hid two-thirds of the time behind some of these accommodating islands. About five o'clock in the afternoon we steam out, and in a most leisurely manner throw a few shells over in the

4

direction of the city. Perhaps we hit the sea-wall in front of the Custom-house; perhaps we hit the heights beyond the town. We knock off for supper, smoke our pipes, fire a few more shells, go back to our anchorage, and — go to sleep. Pshaw! Why, an American naval officer would scare this whole fleet out of the water."

"'Sh-sh! Not so loud. Not that kind of talk. You will be heard; then court-martial. The admiral thinks to tire out the President."

"Well, he'll never tire out Peixoto by plugging those hills full of iron."

"You will see. We shall win yet."

"How is it possible?" demanded Frank. "Here we are, practically penned up in these ships, and unable to get a footing on the land. Every time we try it we are driven back with a considerable loss, and we have no men to spare."

"That will be all right," replied Bennos, confidently. "The land column will march up from Rio Grande do Sul. Then we will win."

Frank shook his head, and gazed gloomily out over the still waters. Bennos laid his hand on the boy's shoulder.

"I know what makes you unhappy," he said, kindly.

"Do you?" said Frank, with awakening interest.

"Yes," continued the Brazilian. "You are not happy because you have no heart in this fight."

"That's true, Roderigo. What difference does it make to me whether we win or not? I've shipped with Admiral Da Gama, and I've taken his money. I've sold myself, and I'll stick to my bargain. My body belongs to the admiral, and I must shed my blood for him if necessary. But what do I care for his success? I'm a miserable hireling. And that is not all."

"No?"

"No. I came down here to look for my missing cousin Robert, and I can get no chance to do anything."

"But you have learned something, *amigo mio*."

"I know that a lad answering his description deserted from the *Tamandare* when she joined the insurgents, and is now in the service of President Peixoto on shore, where I cannot reach him."

"But when we have conquered—"

"I may find his dead body, slain by my companions in arms."

"I am sorry," said Bennos, taking the boy's hand.

At that moment the bugle sounded.

"Ah!" exclaimed Frank. "The usual evening fireworks, eh?"

"Yes; we shall bombard the city some more."

The two young men went to their stations at the 70-pounder Armstrongs. The heavy guns in the turrets were under the command of more experienced officers. Steam was already up, and the *Aquidaban*, followed by three of her consorts in single column at distances of two hundred yards apart, moved slowly and majestically out from the cover of the island. Frank listened with some contempt to the directions of the division officers. He had already learned to understand all the commands in the strange tongue, and he smiled when he heard the range given out.

"Going to pepper the hills again," he said to himself. "Well, this gun of mine is out to hit something before this night's work is done. I'm sick of this fooling."

An American man-of-war's man would have been amused at the leisurely way in which the Brazilians went about the work of warfare, as exemplified in the business of bombarding. Ten minutes after the *Aquidaban* had taken up her position there was a brilliant flash, lighting up all the surrounding waters with a red glare, a deep-mouthed roar, and a rattling jar of the whole ship. Frank peered out of his port.

"That's one of the forward nine-inches," he

muttered, "and I think I know just where to look for the explosion of the shell."

The projectiles of the modern rifles do not leave a trail of fire behind them as they go speeding through the air, because they do not carry the old-fashioned fuse which is lighted by the burning of the powder in the gun. They are exploded by a percussion fuse, and they rush through the darkness of night unseen.

"There she goes," murmured Frank, as he detected a flash of red light far up the hillside behind the city. "They'll have an iron mine up there in the year 1900. Now we'll see the *Republica* plant a shell in the same safe spot."

Boom! The *Republica's* gun spoke, sarcastically commenting on the ship's name by arguing in favor of monarchy.

"That's it," soliloquized Frank. "Same old place. I wonder if the people in the Rua di Ouvidor take off their hats as the shells go over?"

All the members of Frank's gun crew were gathered at the ports watching the firing, so the young man went quietly to the breech of the gun and reduced the range indicated by the breech-sight by 750 yards.

"There," he said to himself. "There's going to be a surprise-party this evening."

The firing continued for half an hour, each ship in turn discharging one gun, before it was Frank's turn. He smiled slightly as he gave the word :

" Fire !"

The gun captain jerked the lanyard, the gun roared, and the 70-pound shell whistled off through the gloom. A few seconds later a dull report, a flash of light, and a crash near the water-front of the city showed that Frank's subtraction had been most accurate. The effect of that telling shot was as if a hornet's nest had been struck. Lights flashed along the water-front and up the hill-side. Tongues of fire shot out far down the bay, followed by heavy reverberating reports, showing that Fort Santa Cruz had opened fire on Fort Villegaignon. Bugles blared and drums rattled, and for half an hour, as the hills hurled the myriad noises back and forth from peak to peak, pandemonium reigned. Then, as suddenly as they had begun, the forts relapsed into a sullen silence. The flashing of lights along the water-front of the city ceased. The order "Cease firing" was signalled from the *Aquidaban* to her consorts, and the three ships moved solemnly back to their anchorage behind the island.

" You are respectfully invited to attend our exhibitions of fireworks every evening from

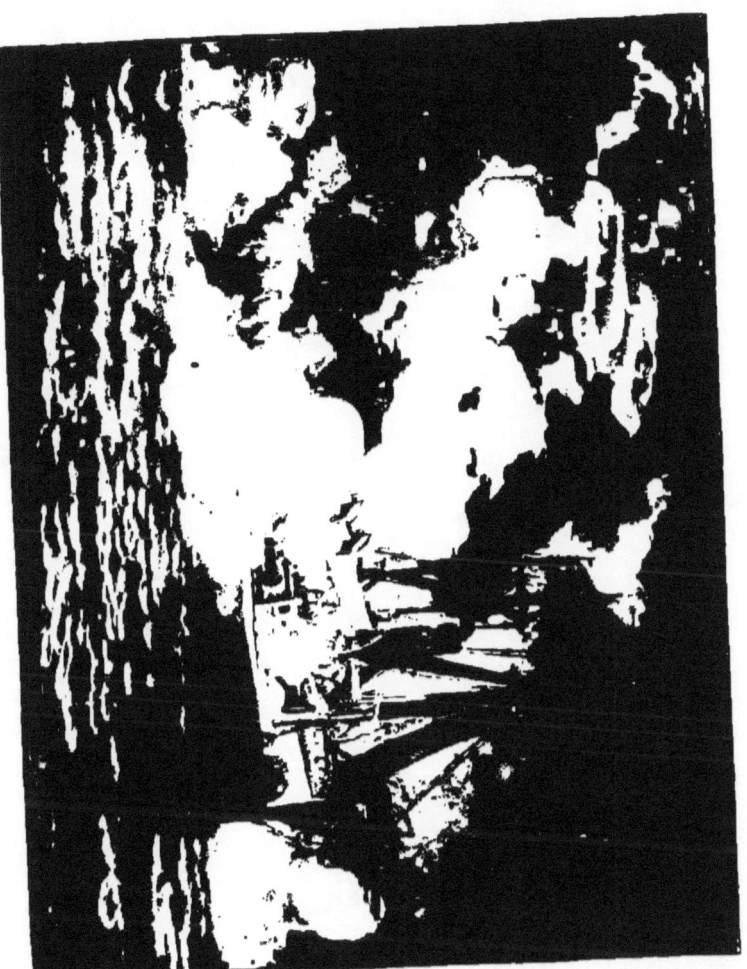

"FIRE!"

nine to ten," said Frank, under his breath, as he watched his crew securing the gun. " Coffee and cigarettes will be served out after the exercises."

The boy shook his head, and added, bitterly :

" I'm an idiot! How could I suppose that I would fight with enthusiasm under a foreign flag? Oh, Harold, old boy, if I had only had you alongside to heave me a line and keep me from going adrift when I was about to ship for Rio!"

" All secure, sir," reported the gun captain, and Frank repeated the report to the division officer. The bugles should have sounded the retreat, but discipline was not stern in the insurgent fleet, and the division officer carelessly commanded Frank to dismiss his crew.

" Leave your quarters," said the boy to his men. Then he went out on deck again and resumed his unprofitable occupation of leaning over the quarter-rail and communing with his own spirit. Fortunately Bennos soon joined him, and led his thoughts into higher channels.

" Come, *amigo mio*," he said. " You must not think any more to-night. We must go below."

They went down to the half-deck, as that part of the gun-deck immediately in front of the wardroom is called, and there they found a gay party of young officers smoking cigarettes, laughing, talking, playing the guitar, and otherwise behaving as if a rebellion against one's country and a night bombardment were holiday amusements. One of the younger men, noting the sober look on Frank's face, began to sing, in badly broken English, "Annie Rooney," which he had learned while the ship was in New York waters. Frank broke into a hearty laugh, and said :

"Oh, I'm going to turn in. Good-night, you fellows. Hope to see you all at the bombardment to-morrow evening."

"Good-night, sharp-shooter!" called one of the young men after him.

Frank was up bright and early the next morning, for he had not yet ceased to enjoy the beauties of the tropical forenoon. Bennos joined him on deck. A few minutes later they observed a good deal of hustling about on some of the foreign war-ships. Men were seen going to the mast-heads, and reports were signalled from one ship to another.

"I wonder what those fellows can see?" said Frank. "Let's get permission from the officer of the deck to go aloft. We can see over the point of the island."

The permission was granted, and the two

young men were soon at the foremast-head. Far down the bay a white ship was cutting the blue waters with slow and steady prow.

Frank gazed at her steadily for a few minutes, and then his face turned pale, while his lips trembled with strong emotion.

"What is the trouble?" asked Bennos.

"Can you not see? Yonder comes the United States cruiser *Charleston*. She is sent here to protect American interests against us — against me! And here am I, enlisted to fight against my own flag!"

"But surely there will be no fighting, *amigo*. There is but one American ship."

"But one! Do you think the government at Washington will stop there? I tell you, Roderigo, there are more ships to follow that one. What have I done with my life?"

CHAPTER IX

THE white ship far down the bay seemed to have stopped her engines. At any rate, she barely kept steerage-way, but just to the northward of Fort Lage she drifted idly. Suddenly Frank saw what looked like a small ball rising to her fore-truck.

"Going to salute the flag of Brazil," said Frank to his companion.

"*Si;* but the forts must answer, not we."

"Of course not. You won't catch the captain of the *Charleston* paying any deference to Admiral Louis Phillipe Saldanha da Gama."

The little ball at the *Charleston's* fore-truck broke out into the green square and yellow diamond of Brazil. At the same instant a streak of blue shot out from her starboard bow and burst into a swirling cloud over the water, while the sharp, incisive report of a Hotchkiss 6-pounder set the tired echoes jumping about the hills once more. The port gun speedily followed the starboard, and the two were fired alternately.

"Twenty-one," said Frank, "and fired as if by clock-work. That's not an admiral's salute, Bennos."

"The *Charleston* does not salute us."

"Ah!" exclaimed Frank; "there goes old Santa Cruz in reply. Oh, glory! what a salute! It sounds as if the fort were lame."

"I think she is," said Bennos, smiling.

"The Brazilian flag is stowed away in the quartermaster's locker by this time," said Frank. "Now the ship is coming on up the bay."

It was such a calm, clear morning that there was no difficulty whatever in detecting the smother of foam under her bows, which told that her speed had increased.

"She's a sweet ship," said Frank, with pride. "I fell in love with her when I saw her in New York Harbor. She looks like a fighter."

"*Si, si, amigo mio,*" said Bennos, warmly; "that's a good ship."

"But not as good as the *Aquidaban*, eh?"

"No, not that good."

"No, she hasn't any armor, and her guns are lighter than ours. But I'll tell you one thing, Roderigo."

"What's that?" inquired Bennos, with interest.

"She'd hit us a heap oftener than we'd hit her."

"You could hit her," said the Brazilian, significantly.

"Yes, I *could* hit her," said Frank.

"And you would, eh?"

Frank turned a trifle pale under his sunburn as he answered:

"What's the use of talking about that, Roderigo? You know that there isn't going to be any fighting between the American ship and any of ours."

"No, the American will not fight. He will let a foreigner insult his flag. We Brazilians would rather die!"

Frank made no reply to this, for it would have been useless. It would have been impossible to persuade Bennos that an American commander might be found who would take the responsibility of using powder and shot without waiting for permission from Washington, or that the national government would support any such officer if he were found. We Americans are very boastful; but the foreign powers—even the small Central American states—have not had much respect for our flag until very lately.

"I wonder where she's going to anchor," said Frank.

"Up the bay, near the other foreign ships. She must keep out of the line of fire."

"Yes, and a good way out of it, too. If she isn't astern of us when we open up with our batteries, she's very likely to get thumped."

"You do not like the way we shoot?"

"We can't shoot at all in this fleet, Roderigo. Why, my class at the Naval Academy could have given lessons to your gunners."

Bennos smiled a good-natured smile, and turned his attention to the *Charleston*. She was now above Cobras Island, and was still steaming ahead at a six-knot gait. Frank's heart beat with mingled emotions of pride and grief as he got his first fair look at the stars and stripes floating over the taffrail.

"Alas, for my folly!" he muttered. "I ought to be afloat with that flag, not with this."

Bennos overheard his words.

"I do not blame you for feeling so," he said.

A few minutes later the *Charleston* ranged abreast of the *Aquidaban*. Frank straightened himself up as he stood in the top, and raised his cap.

"What is that for?" asked his companion.

"I salute the flag of my country, which I ought to be serving," replied Frank.

"That is right," said Bennos.

"Right!" exclaimed Frank. "Are you serving your country's flag, or are you a rebel?"

"I fight for the best. I want my country to have an emperor. A republic is not good here."

"Roderigo, I ask your pardon. I know you are enlisted in what you believe to be the right cause."

The two young men were again silent for a few minutes as they watched the *Charleston*. Then, for some unaccountable reason, Frank turned his gaze towards the entrance to the harbor.

"Look!" he cried, pointing.

Bennos followed the injunction, and saw a noble bark-rigged white cruiser coming in between the forts.

"I know her!" exclaimed Frank. "The *Newark!*"

"Four thousand tons; twelve 6-inch guns," said Bennos.

"Uncle Sam means business," said Frank, exultingly.

"Only two," said Bennos, smiling.

At that moment they were hailed from the deck, and at once descended from the top. An orderly handed Frank a letter, which he eagerly opened. As he glanced over it his face became clouded.

"You have bad news?" asked Bennos.

"I hardly know," answered Frank. "My un-

cle and cousin are coming to Rio in search of
Bob. I am afraid Uncle Hiram will find this a
troublesome port for an American merchant
vessel."

CHAPTER X

THE "DETROIT" COMES TO ANCHOR

WE left the *Detroit* plunging over the swell left by a southeasterly gale. We meet her again sailing through an enchanted ocean on a fine tropical winter morning. She was alone on the unruffled bosom of the South Atlantic, for as far as the eye could see there was nothing else in sight save sky, water, and a few birds wheeling across the burnished waste. The cruiser was reeling off ten knots an hour with the regularity of clock-work. Her clean white sides were reflected in grotesque distortion in the ribbon-like waves that streamed sternward from her cutting prow, where the lucent blue broke into fountains of silver that leaped almost to her hawse-holes. She rolled slowly and gently, and as she swayed the sunlight came and went in gay flashes along the slender chases of the broadside guns, which seemed to peer out of the ports like living creatures sniffing the strange airs. A canopy of light-brown smoke spread from the tall yellow stacks far away astern and made shadows on the sea,

out of which an occasional flying-fish sprang with
a silver flash like a shooting-star.   The sun beat
down upon the decks with a heat that would
have been distressing had it not been for the
breeze the vessel's progress created.

Mr. Burrell was pacing up and down the
bridge with his hands behind his back, his dark-
blue uniform making his form stand out in sharp
silhouette against the bright sky.   The man at
the wheel stood stolidly gazing into the compass-
bowl and occasionally giving the spokes an apparently careless twist; but the broad, straight
path of foam astern told that he was holding
the ship to her course.   A dozen or more white-
garbed figures sprawled in the sun on the forecastle - deck, while under the awning on the
quarter-deck several officers sat enjoying the
breeze.   The marine on duty as orderly before
the cabin door looked uncomfortable in spite of
the summery appearance of his white helmet
and duck trousers.   The rescued sailor had been
transferred to a steamer bound for New York.
George Briscomb was walking up and down the
starboard waist; and Harold King was leaning
against the forestay, looking straight ahead, and
letting his eyes feast on the splendid blue of the
tropical sea.   The whole ship's company had an
air of indolence, as if smitten by the languor of

5

the southern clime, and a touch of fitting sentiment was added by the mellow tones of a negro
sailor's voice singing "'Way Rio." But just as
the kiss of the Prince in *The Sleeping Beauty*
threw the whole slumbering castle into a clatter
of wakeful action, so a sudden clear and musical
cry from aloft swept away the languor, and
strained to alert tension every figure aboard the
ship.

" Land, ho !"

" Where away ?" cried Mr. Burrell.

" A point off the starboard bow, sir," came the
answer.

Harold straightened up and sent a keen gaze
forward. The sprawling figures on the forecastle-
deck sprang to their feet and looked ahead.
The man at the wheel forgot the compass-bowl.
The officers on the poop-deck ran to the rails on
either side. George sprang to the platform of
one of the Hotchkiss 6-pounders. Every eye
on the ship was gazing eagerly ahead. The
door of the navigator's room swung open, and
Mr. Flower hastened to the bridge.

" That should be the mountain-tops on Flora
Point in range with Pai Island," said he. " The
captain laid the course to pass outside of the
island, and I got a Sumner line early this morning bearing for the westerly end of it."

Commander Brownson now came forward and mounted the bridge. " How far away are the mountains ?" he asked.

" About forty-three miles, according to the time they were sighted from the mast-head, sir," answered Mr. Flower.

" And how does that agree with our reckoning ?"

" Pretty well, sir," answered the navigator. " We are perhaps five miles nearer to the coast than we thought."

" Hum ; but as I laid the course so well out we have run into no danger. We shall be up with Pai Island in four hours or a little more. How far is it thence to the entrance of the harbor ?"

" Four miles nor'west by nor'," answered Mr. Flower, " with nothing less than seven fathoms."

" Mr. Crane will take the bridge when we are abreast of the island," said the commander, turning to descend from the bridge.

" Very good, sir," said Mr. Flower. " Mr. King."

" Aye, aye, sir," answered Harold, starting suddenly from his position near the foot of the forestay.

" Go to the mast-head and tell me what you see."

"Aye, aye, sir," replied the boy, with one foot already on the sheer-pole. His lithe form sprang up the ratlines, and in a few seconds he was in the top.

"Hills, sir," he called, "and plenty of them on both bows, with a narrow opening dead ahead of us. It looks as if it might be a river's mouth, sir."

"Where do you find the highest point?"

"Just clear of the starboard bow, sir."

"Let me know when it is dead ahead. Port a little." The last injunction was to the man at the helm.

"Meet her, sir, meet her," cried Harold. "Now, steady as you are, sir."

"Very good. Lay down from aloft."

"Aye, aye, sir," was the boy's reply, as he dropped down the ratlines like a young cat.

"The high peak will be in direct range with the westerly end of Pai Island," said Mr. Flower to Mr. Burrell. "Keep the ship heading for it till you raise the island, and then call me."

Mr. Flower went below, and a few minutes later, when four bells struck and George went to the chart-house to make his entries in the log, the blue mountain-peak was visible from the bridge.

"The rift in the hills that Harold reported

will be the entrance to Rio Harbor, won't it?"
asked George, after making his report to Mr.
Burrell.

"Yes; and we shall be at anchor with the
Charleston and *Newark* this afternoon."

George went aft, thinking a little more seriously than was his custom. "Frank is there, I suppose," he reflected, "aboard the *Aquidaban*. I
wonder how he likes foreign service?"

At a quarter of two o'clock Pai Island, with
its bosky hills rising 325 feet above the sea, was
on the *Detroit's* starboard beam. Mr. Crane and
Mr. Flower appeared on the bridge, and the
latter stretched the chart of Rio Harbor on the
chart-board. Harold and George were off duty,
but they remained on deck to enjoy the glorious
beauties of the entrance to the harbor. As the
cruiser passed up the bay George said: "I don't
see anything of any war-ships."

"Neither do I."

The same thing had just occurred to the group
of officers on the bridge. They were anxiously
scanning the short stretch of water between
Villegaignon and Cobras islands, set down on
the chart as the anchorage for men-of-war, but
it was clear.

"They've gone farther up the bay, to be out of
the range of firing," said Commander Brownson.

"Here they are!" exclaimed Mr. Burrell.

"And there's the *Charleston!*" said Mr. Flower.

"With signals flying. Here, Mr. King," called Mr. Crane, turning and catching sight of Harold, "bring my signal-book as quickly as possible."

Harold sprang to obey the command, and was on the bridge with the blue-covered book in a few seconds. Mr. Burrell took a look at the flags on the *Charleston* through his glass. In the meantime the quartermaster on watch had got the answering pennant from the locker, and had bent it on the signal halyards ready to run up.

"Two-thirty-seven," said Mr. Burrell, lowering the glass.

"Anchor in column," read Harold from the book.

"Run up your pennant," said Mr. Burrell.

A quarter of an hour later the *Detroit* lay at anchor.

"Look, Hal. Look!" exclaimed George. "Yonder lies the rebel fleet."

"And there's the *Aquidaban!* I wonder if we shall see Frank?"

"Them as doesn't see folks sometimes hears 'em," remarked Cockswain Morris, who was passing.

"'WHAT IS TO BE DONE WITH ME NOW?'"

"Talking of hearing," said George, " I wonder if Frank has heard anything of Robert."

At that very moment a tall, bronzed young man, with reddish-brown hair and dark eyes, was pacing up and down a narrow cell in a prison in Rio. A rattling of bolts warned him that he was about to receive a visit from his captors. The door swung open, and an officer entered, while four soldiers halted outside.

"Come!" said the officer.

"What is to be done with me now?" asked the young man, impatiently. "Haven't I told you over and over again that I'm no spy; that I deserted from the *Tamandare* as soon as she joined the rebels, and came ashore to offer myself to the government service?"

"We have other information," said the officer; "and now we are told that plans are being made for your escape. You are to be taken to another place of confinement."

The boy said no more, but marched out between the soldiers. He was blindfolded and handcuffed, placed in a vehicle, and driven over several miles of rough road. When he was left alone in his new prison he peered out between the bars, and saw that he was somewhere among the hills back of the city.

"I suppose I shall stay here till the war is over, if they don't take a notion to shoot me," he muttered, as he buried his face in his hands.

CHAPTER XI

THE THREE FRIENDS MEET

"Mr. King!"

"Aye, aye, sir."

Harold was superintending some slight work on the forecastle-deck when he was called by Mr. Harniss.

"I want you and Mr. Briscomb to take the second cutter in tow of the launch, and go to the wharf to bring off some stores."

"Very good, sir," said Harold.

A few minutes later the boats were alongside. Harold jumped into the steam-launch, and took in tow the cutter, with George in the stern-sheets. Neither boat carried a full crew, but had just enough men to handle them in case of emergency. All available space and carrying power was reserved for the stores to be brought off. The strong, chubby little launch pulled the heavy cutter along at a lively pace, and as the foam rolled past them, and their speed created a refreshing breeze, the two boys recovered from a depression which had settled upon them during the days of dull routine drill and work subsequent to their arrival. It was the first time they had secured an opportunity to go ashore. Liberty was not often given, on account of the unsettled condition of affairs in the city. American seamen were especially liable to assault by the disaffected elements of the populace, because there was a suppressed but general feeling that in some way the power of the United States would sooner or later make itself felt in the struggle. Harold and George understood the condition of affairs, and they were careful not to permit their men to leave the wharf. Their stores having been obtained, they got under way again for the ship. As they were passing the point of the island near which the insurgent fleet was anchored, they saw a whale-boat urged over the smooth water by brawny dark arms. An officer stood in the stern, waving his hand.

"Say, Hal," called George from the cutter, "I do believe that's Frank."

"So do I," answered Hal.

"Well, we must stop and have a few minutes' chat with him, old man."

"Yes, of course. We are away inside of the time we were allowed for getting these stores."

It was Frank. He had been walking the deck of the *Aquidaban* when his eye chanced to fall

on the two boats of the *Detroit* passing the point.
Knowing the ways of the American navy, he
supposed that they would be in charge of cadets, and of course there was a chance that the
cadets might be his friends. So he ran to the
quartermaster on duty, and borrowed his binocular. The moment he levelled the glass at the
boats he saw that the two young officers in
them were Harold and George. He went at
once to the executive officer of the ship, and said :

"Two boats from the American cruiser *Detroit* have just gone ashore. They are in command of two classmates and dear friends of
mine. I'd like very much to speak to them, but
of course they can't come aboard. Will you give
me permission to go off in a boat and speak to
them as they are returning?"

It has already been intimated that discipline
was by no means perfect in the rebel fleet.
Moreover, the executive officer had eaten a
very hearty dinner, and was sleepy. So he replied :

"Oh, certainly. Go on."

Frank reported the matter to the officer of the
deck, and the boat was at once ordered away.
As it approached the two boats from the *Detroit*, Harold brought them to a rest. A minute later all three boats were drifting together.

"Well, this is a jolly go!" exclaimed George, as he shook Frank's hand. "Who would have thought that we three fellows would meet in Rio Harbor?"

"I never expected to see you fellows down here," said Frank; "but I'm mighty glad that you're here."

"We are not so tremendously glad about it," said Hal.

"Why?" asked Frank.

"Because we are here to help protect American interests, and I understand they are in more danger from the reb — from Admiral Da Gama than from President Peixoto."

"That may be so," said Frank, "but what difference does that make to you?"

"Why, Frank," exclaimed George, "we might have to fight against you."

Frank hung his head and looked sad.

"You didn't think of that possibility when you enlisted in this service, did you, Frank?" asked Hal.

"No, of course not. If I had I shouldn't have enlisted."

"Besides," said George, "the chances are that there will not be any trouble."

"There ought to be," said Frank.

"Why?" asked both the others.

"Because the flag of the United States means nothing to these people down here. I've seen it insulted half a dozen times since I've been here by the man under whom I am serving. I am almost tempted to desert."

"But you wouldn't do that!" exclaimed Harold, at the same time glancing inquiringly at the Brazilian seamen.

"Never mind them," said Frank. "They don't understand a word of anything except Portuguese and Spanish. But why should I not desert, rather than see my country's flag insulted?"

"Because you have pledged yourself to serve under the insurgent flag. Your word must not be broken," said Harold.

"But you might resign," suggested George.

"That would look like running away," said Hal.

"Not if he explained his reasons," said George.

"No, it wouldn't work," said Frank. "They wouldn't accept my resignation. Educated naval officers are too scarce, Bennos says."

"Bennos? Is that the one we met in New York?"

"Yes; and you've no idea what a good fellow he is. He has almost made life endurable for me aboard yonder ship."

"Remember us both to him, Frank," said Hal, "and give him our kindest regards."

"What's that?" exclaimed George.

The deep reverberation of a gun rolled up the bay, followed by another, and yet others. All hands turned their gaze southward, where they beheld a white ship with a three-masted schooner rig coming up the bay.

"What ship is that?" asked Frank.

"Don't you remember her?" cried Hal; "that's the *San Francisco*. She was not expected till next week."

"That makes four ships for Uncle Sam in Rio Harbor," said George.

"Yet there is no match for my prison there," said Frank, nodding towards the *Aquidaban*.

"That's true enough," said Hal; "but the *Aquidaban* may not always be lying at anchor in Rio Harbor. She may have to go elsewhere."

"I hope and pray that she may do so, if there is to be trouble with the United States fleet."

The three boys sat silently watching the *San Francisco* as she came speedily up the bay. When she was opposite the *Aquidaban* she ran up the Brazilian flag and saluted it. The officers of the insurgent flag-ship seemed somewhat taken aback, but they contrived to reply within reasonable time.

"HAROLD AND GEORGE STOOD UP AT ATTENTION."

"Well," said George, "that doesn't look as if there was going to be trouble."

"I am afraid it does," said Hal; "trouble for Admiral Stanton, who's in command of the *San Francisco* and now, also, of our fleet. I shouldn't be surprised if Uncle Sam invited him to come home."

"Then you don't think the government at Washington will recognize — us," said Frank, putting a bitter emphasis on the last word.

"I'm afraid not, Frank," said Harold. "Our government is committed to the friendly support of republics."

Bang! went another gun down the bay. This time all three boys sprang to their feet, for all were thoroughly surprised.

"It's a white ship!" exclaimed George. "A big one!"

Harold had a pair of marine glasses, and he raised them to his eyes.

"The American flag!" he exclaimed.

"Then it's the armored cruiser *New York!*" cried George. "Frank, old man, the *Aquidaban* will find her an ugly customer!"

"I pray not," said Frank, sadly.

"Poor old man!" exclaimed Harold, sympathetically.

The three boys now silently watched the mag-

nificent war-ship steaming in majestic state up
the harbor. Through his glasses Harold could
see that the water-fronts of Rio and Nictheroy
were black with people waving their hats and
handkerchiefs. The rigging of the British men-
of-war looked like a lot of spider-webs well
stocked with flies, while the decks of the other
war-ships were crowded with sailor-men gazing
eagerly at the latest example of Uncle Sam's
new navy. The American merchantmen manned
their yards and ran up all their flags, while across
the waters came ringing three hearty Yankee
cheers. The cruiser dipped her flag in answer
to all these tokens of welcome, and steered steadily for the anchorage indicated by the *San Francisco's* signals. With her three yellow stacks,
her two turrets showing the four 8-inch guns,
her frowning broadside of 4-inch rapid-fire guns,
and her double fighting-tops, she looked a picture
of naval prowess. As she glided by the launch
and the two cutters within a biscuit's throw,
Harold and George stood up at attention, their
hearts beating high, while they read across her
rounded stern the words "*New York*."

CHAPTER XII

AN ALARMING OUTLOOK

"W'ich the same I begs your pardon, sir," said Peter Morris, who was acting as cockswain of the launch, "but as my brother Bill used to say, clocks 'ain't got no patience, an' won't wait."

"That's so, Peter," said Hal; "we must be moving back to the ship."

"Wait a minute," said Frank. "I've not told you my most important news yet."

"I thought you had something on your mind," said George.

"It's about your cousin Bob," added Hal.

"Partly, and also about my uncle Hiram and Minnie."

"What is it, Frank?" asked George.

"Have you learned anything about your cousin?" inquired Hal.

"Wait a bit, fellows, and I'll tell you the whole of it. I find now that I was doubly foolish in enlisting in this service. Not only am I serving a foreign flag, but I am practically a prisoner on the water. As far as I can ascertain,

6

my cousin Robert—if our man is really he—deserted from the *Tamandare* when the rebellion broke out, and is now in the service of Peixoto. I can't go ashore to make a single move in the search for him, because I am an officer in the rebel fleet. And even if I could, I shouldn't know what to do with him if I found him, for Bennos tells me the insurgent admiral would have him shot for deserting."

"Well, old man, that's pretty rough," said Hal.

"It are wot we calls afore the mast," said Peter, "hangin' atwixt wind an' water."

Frank looked inquiringly at Hal, who said:

"Cockswain Peter Morris is a privileged character with us; he saved our lives in Norfolk Harbor."

Frank shook hands with the honest seaman, and then continued:

"I wrote to Uncle Hiram telling him all about this matter, and three days ago I received his reply."

"What did he say?" asked Hal.

"Well, the fact is," answered Frank, "he's coming down here."

"What, to Rio!" exclaimed George.

"Yes; he can't stand the anxiety any longer," said Frank, "and he's coming down to try and carry on the search himself."

Frank drew the letter from his pocket and handed it to his two friends. It had been forwarded from one of the West-Indian islands, and read thus:

"DEAR FRANK,—You will be surprised, I know, when you read this letter, for I write to tell you that I am about to start for Rio, where I expect to meet you. Captain Bisbee, of my bark, the *Alma*, has been taken sick, and will be unable to go out this voyage. So I am taking advantage of the situation to command the bark myself, and so go down to Rio to see if I can't do something about finding my boy. If what you tell me is true, I sha'n't have so very much trouble about finding him, though I may not be able to get him released from the government service right away. Still, from what I read in the papers, the rebellion don't amount to much, and will soon be over. I've made up my mind to bring Minnie along with me. I haven't any one to leave her with, and I haven't the heart to put her in a boarding-school. So, as the *Alma* has about as tidy a cabin as any clipper-ship that sails out of New York, she's going to be my passenger. So when you get this letter, Frank, I'll be taking a squint to windward once more, and heading for low latitudes with as fine a keel

under me as ever was laid. Minnie sends you
her love.   Your affectionate uncle,

"HIRAM LOCKWOOD.

"P.S.—We are lying at anchor at St. Thomas,
and I just found this letter in one of my pockets.
I thought I'd sent it long ago. We fell in with
a hard puff from the no'theast the other day, and
carried away our flying jib-boom. So I made St.
Thomas to get another. I'm going to send this
letter by the steamer that leaves to-day. Minnie's learning to be a right good sailor, and before we get home I reckon she'll be able to keep
her weather eye lifting with the best of them."

"What a brave, cheerful man he is in spite of
his trouble!" said Hal, warmly.

"Yes, he is, God bless him!" said Frank.
"But I wish he knew the exact condition of affairs down here."

"Is it so bad for the merchant ships?" asked
George.

"If you weren't just cadets," said Frank, a
little impatiently, "you'd know what was going
on. Merchant ships in this harbor haven't had
any protection at all. Our gunners are rank,
and there have been some pretty wild shots that
must have scraped the varnish off some of their

spars. Worse than that, I don't think our officers care a rap if we do hit a bark or two. England's the only power we're afraid of, and we think she sympathizes with us. But there's something else. Have you noticed the wharves?"

"Yes," replied Harold. "They're all unoccupied."

"And the merchant ships," continued Frank, "are spending a lot of money on lighters to land their cargoes. That's because Admiral Da Gama refuses to let the ships go to the wharves, for when they are there he can't fire on the city on account of their being in the line of fire."

"I hadn't thought of that," said Harold.

"No," said Frank, "and I didn't pay much attention to it myself till I got this letter. Now I know Uncle Hiram. He will not come down here without a cargo; and he'll insist on going to a wharf. Besides, he must be in constant communication with the city if he's going to find Bob; and so—"

The boy's speech was rudely interrupted by the shriek of a shot passing over the boats.

"Give 'way, lads!" he cried; "it's one of the government's armed tugs, and she's after me."

"How dare they fire on our flag?" exclaimed George.

"W'ich the same they didn't," said Peter;

" 'cos w'y : I took it down.   It are jest as well to
keep dark w'en you are a-conwarsin' with rebels."

"But they'll catch him," said Hal.   "He has
half a mile the start, but his men can't row him
fast enough."

"W'en in doubt play trumps are wot I says,"
said Peter.   " Let's go an' give him a tow."

It was a hazardous thing to do, for if the boys
had been detected by their superiors they would
have been liable to court - martial for "taking
sides" in the quarrel.   But they did not stop to
think of that.   The little launch puffed away,
and soon overtook Frank's boat.

"Give us your painter, old man!" cried George;
"we'll tow you close to the *Aquidaban*."

The line was taken, and the launch began to
tow the two cutters.

"They're a-gainin' on to us," said Peter; "but
a starn chase are a long chase, as the plough
said to the farmer."

At this instant a heavy report rang out, and a
shot from the *Aquidaban* whizzed across the
bows of the tug.

"I reckon that'll take four knots off her
speed," said Peter, looking back over his shoulder.

"Edge her off towards the point yonder,
Peter," said Harold.   "We must not be seen
from the decks of any of our ships."

" Werry good, sir, but that are a course w'ch 'll keep the tug out o' the *Aquidaban's* range."

" Never mind that. We can go ashore if we're hard pressed."

The chase now became exciting. The tug was gaining on the three small boats, and was firing rapidly. Shots were falling all around the boats, but fortunately none struck them. The course which Harold had indicated was gradually placing a point of the island of Engenha between the fugitives and the rebel war-ships.

" I'm afraid you've missed it, Hal," said George. " They're gaining on us."

At that moment the Brazilians in Frank's boat gave a cheer, and the light cruiser *Trajano* was seen moving out from her anchorage behind the point. She fired two shots, and the government tug turned tail and puffed away towards the city. The boys shook hands and separated, Frank's crew pulling leisurely back to the *Aquidaban*, while the two cadets made a wide détour and approached the American fleet from another quarter.

CHAPTER XIII

CAPTAIN LOCKWOOD'S WARM RECEPTION

ABOUT the same time a fat brown rooster poked his head out of a coop on the deck of a vessel flying over the sea towards Rio, and loosed a lusty crow.

"Dat's a berry fine woice yo's got, chile, but yo' don't sing no moah in dese hyah latitoods."

And Kibo, the cook, plunged his arm into the coop and dragged the struggling, squawking victim forth.

"Hi yah! He bully fat!" exclaimed Kibo. And then he began to sing :

> "Hoop te loo loo ! W'at's de mattah ?
> Flap yo' wings an' kick yo' feet ;
> Fry 'im in de grease an' battah ;
> Cracky! but 'im good to eat !"

"Belay that jaw tackle there, you blathering heathen, and get at your foul-smelling cookery !"

Captain Lockwood's voice scraped along the deck with a rumble like a chain-cable. His land manners had slipped from him like an old wrapper, and he was a sturdy, deep-chested, hump-shouldered old sea-dog, with a blazing red face and a jolly gray eye. He balanced himself on his columnar legs, and from a station near the foot of the mizzen-mast he let his gaze slowly roam over the swelling curves of white canvas that towered away through double tops and top-gallants to the naked royal-yards. The fresh breeze abeam was heeling the *Alma* down till the water boiled and hissed around her lee chan-nels. The long South Atlantic surges were toss-ing their hoary heads high in air as they raced down upon the bark, and ever and anon as she plunged down a foaming steep she would hurl a sheet of green water into shivers of smoky spray across her forecastle-deck.

" Oh, she's a sweet lady to smoke through it, isn't she, Minnie?" said the captain, as his daughter appeared on deck.

" Yes, indeed, papa. What is she making?"

" A good twelve, I'll be bound," said the skip-per, taking a squint over the side.

" Twelve it is, sir, by the last heave," said the mate.

" It's simply glorious!" exclaimed Minnie.

The girl looked a picture of healthy enjoy-ment. Her wavy hair streamed in pretty dis-order around her well-tanned cheeks, and her eyes sparkled like stars.

"We must be raising the land pretty fast at that gait," said the captain.

"Yes, sir," answered the mate. "You can see it plain enough from the forecastle."

Land had been sighted some time before, and the bark was ratching along with the Brazilian mountains peering over the sea under her lee bow.

"But we'll have to clew up our top-gallants if this breeze freshens any," said the skipper. "There's a bit too much weight in that sea."

"Oh, I hope not!" said Minnie. "I love to see the bark lie down to her work and toss the spray this way. She seems to be alive."

"That's a real sailor's daughter," said the mate, laughing.

"By faith, she'd carry the masts out of a ship if she was the captain," said her father, smiling. "Clew up, Mr. Ball; we'll do as well under shorter canvas."

"Aye, aye, sir," said the mate, and the next minute he was bawling orders that caused the two roaring stretches of canvas away aloft to fold their white wings. The bark was now on an easier keel, but she seemed to go quite as fast; and within three hours she had Flora Point on her starboard bow.

"Oh, how wonderful! How glorious!" exclaimed Minnie, as she stood, with clasped hands and parted lips, gazing at the rich green mountain slopes.

"I knew you'd like it," said the captain. "I'm glad I brought you, Minnie."

"So am I," she answered.

Captain Lockwood pointed out to her the various beauties of the harbor, the forts and the islands, as the bark, under shortened canvas, sailed slowly past Fort Lage. The vessel was full of the busy rattle of blocks as the men made her ready for coming to anchor.

"Yonder lies Villegaignon Island," said the captain. "We'll run pretty close along there, and you'll get a good look at the fort. Let her luff a little!"

"Luff it is, sir," answered the man at the wheel.

The bark glided under the walls of the fort, and suddenly a voice rang across the water:

"Keep off!"

Captain Lockwood sprang to the weather-rail and shouted:

"What's the matter? Are we doing any harm?"

His reply was a puff of smoke, followed by the sharp crack of a rifle, and a bullet whistled across the deck.

"Go below, Minnie!" exclaimed the captain, thrusting his daughter towards the cabin door. Then he sprang on the rail and bellowed:

"You miserable scoundrel! I'll make your rebel skin sweat for this!"

A derisive laugh rang out from the caissons, and another shot was fired, the bullet this time cutting a small round hole in the tack of the spanker.

"Well, this beats the Dutch!" exclaimed Captain Lockwood, as the bark slipped out of range on her way up the bay.

"It seems to me, sir," said the mate, "that the rebels are running things in a pretty high-handed style down here."

"I should say so. But you can make up your mind to one thing, Mr. Ball."

"Yes, sir; what's that?"

"I'll not sit still and be shot at on my own peaceable decks. I'll carry this business to somebody that 'll have a word to say about it if I have to go all the way to Washington."

"Bark ahoy!"

"Hello! What now?"

A tug manned by insurgents ran alongside, and Captain Lockwood was informed that he would have to anchor his vessel out in the bay and lighter his cargo ashore. He was told that

"'I'LL MAKE YOUR REBEL SKIN SWEAT FOR THIS!'"

any attempt to take his vessel to one of the city wharfs would call forth fire from the insurgents.

"Well, this is about as big an outrage as I ever met with!" stormed the captain.

"You understand?" called the insurgent.

"Oh yes, I understand," answered Captain Lockwood. "But I'm going to obey under protest."

The insurgent replied to the effect that he did not care a pinch of snuff about the protest. All he desired was obedience.

"Well, I'm going to apply to your admiral the first thing to-morrow for permission to go to a wharf," shouted the captain. "I have been fired on by your people, and that's a piece of cowardice."

The insurgent intimated that calling his friends cowards did them no harm, and that Admiral Da Gama would probably decline to see the captain of the bark *Alma*.

"We'll see about that to-morrow," answered the captain. "Get away from alongside now, and give me room to bring my bark to anchor."

With jeering laughter ringing from her decks, the insurgent tug steamed away, and Captain Lockwood roared, in a voice of thunder:

"Clew up the fore and main tops'ls! Haul

down the jib! Haul out the spanker! Down
with your helm!"

A few minutes later the crashing rattle of the
cable passing through the hawse-hole told that
the *Alma* had come to anchor in six fathoms,
half a mile to the northward and westward of
Cobras Island.

CHAPTER XIV

MIGHT AGAINST RIGHT

THE next morning was cloudy and sultry, and Captain Lockwood, after a quick survey of the heavens, expressed it as his belief that there would be a tropical thunder-storm before midnight.

"Look to our starboard anchor, Mr. Ball, and see all ready to let go," he said, "for these squalls come very suddenly and blow very hard in Rio Harbor."

"Aye, aye, sir," said Mr. Ball. "A pair of mudhooks make a good storm-stays'l, they do."

"And see my boat in ship-shape order, Mr. Ball," continued the captain. "I'm going to do myself the honor of making a call on Admiral Da Gama this morning."

"There's a man-o'-war's boat a-comin', sir," said a sailor.

"With the American flag flying," added the captain, picking up his glass and levelling it. "Why, it's Hal King and George Briscomb."

The two boys were soon aboard the bark, and

explained how they had obtained permission to call on their friends.

"Have you seen Frank?" asked Minnie, anxiously.

"Yes," answered Harold; and then he proceeded to give a complete account of their meeting with their friend, and their conversation with him about Robert.

"That makes it all the more necessary that I should get the bark alongside a city wharf where I can be in easy communication with the government officials," said Captain Lockwood. "I've got to see this boy that deserted from the *Tumandare*, and if it's Robert, I must get him out of this service and home. I don't care to stay in Rio Harbor any longer than I've got to after my reception."

The boys looked at him inquiringly.

"Oh, you haven't heard about it, eh?" he asked, and then he told them the story which aroused them to a state of indignation. They feared, however, that nothing would be accomplished by a visit to the insurgent admiral.

"But it's worth trying, sir," said Hal. "It would be a dreadful thing if the American fleet had to enforce your demand, for we should have to fight against Frank and he against your rights."

" This is going to be a serious business before we're through with it," said the captain; " but I owe a duty to my fellow-mariners, and if it comes to a question between my son and my nephew, why, Frank must play second fiddle."

After a little further conversation the boys departed, having assured Captain Lockwood that they would give him every assistance in their power in the search for his son. The captain paced the deck for half an hour in deep thought, and then spoke in a decisive manner:

" I shall go to this insurgent admiral, and put my case plainly to him."

" But you won't tell him about Robert ?" said Minnie.

" No, that wouldn't do. But I must get to a wharf. Mr. Ball, get my boat alongside."

The order was obeyed, and in a few minutes Captain Lockwood was speeding across the bay behind four sturdy oarsmen of his crew. The flag of Admiral Da Gama had been transferred to the wooden corvette *Libertade*, and Captain Lockwood took his boat alongside her starboard accommodation-ladder, where he was received with considerable surprise by the tall, dark-skinned marine on sentry duty. Nevertheless, he was permitted to board the ship, while his boat was sent to lie at the boom. The officer of

r

the deck sent a messenger to inform the commanding officer of the captain's desire. In a few minutes the man returned, and said that the admiral would see the American captain. Entering the cabin of the *Libertade*, Captain Lockwood found himself in the presence of a keen-eyed, saturnine man, with a set, inexpressive countenance. He was sitting bolt-upright behind a table, with both hands resting upon it at arm's-length. His air and attitude were full of supercilious conceit, and Captain Lockwood could scarcely forbear a smile.

"To what do I owe the honor of this visit?" asked the admiral, speaking with a slight accent and a sneering manner.

"I have come, sir," replied Captain Lockwood, calmly, "to ask your permission to lay my bark alongside one of the city wharves. Discharging cargo by the aid of lighters is a very expensive business, as you must know, sir."

"I do know," said the admiral, bowing slightly, "but you must discharge your cargo that way. I cannot grant your request."

"May I ask why?"

"Yes. You cannot lie at a wharf without being in my line of fire. I must be free to fire upon the city when I choose without danger of injuring foreign ships, and so embroiling myself with foreign powers."

"But—pardon me, admiral—don't you think you are just as likely to get yourself into trouble by preventing vessels from landing?"

"I have prevented them, and no trouble has come," said the admiral, with a cold smile. "I shall continue to do so."

"By what right?"

"By the right which I have created," answered Admiral Da Gama, impressively. "The navy of Brazil has thrown off the yoke of the tyrant Peixoto, and is fighting for the freedom of the land. Here, upon the water, our war-ships are the supreme ruling power. My plans must not be disturbed, and I shall not permit them to be."

"Then your right is simply might."

"Call it that, if it pleases you."

Captain Lockwood was silent for a moment, and then he said:

"Was it by your orders that my bark was fired upon in entering the harbor?"

"Yes," said the admiral, smiling.

"I protest against it as an outrage."

"You may protest till you are hoarse, sir, but it will be in vain. I have established a blockade on the water-front of Rio de Janeiro, and the shots were fired simply as a warning. They could not have harmed you. They were blank-cartridges."

"I never before heard the whistle of a bullet follow the discharge of a blank-cartridge."

"All imagination," said the admiral, hastily. "There were no bullets—though I cannot say what might happen if you attempted to go to the wharf."

"Am I to understand that this is a threat?"

"I do not threaten merchantmen," replied Admiral Da Gama, coldly. "I order them, and they obey."

"I deny your right to order me."

"Your denial will not help you, sir. Understand once and for all that you are forbidden to take your vessel to a wharf, and that if you do attempt it you will be stopped by my ships."

"I thank you, sir, for the politeness with which you have received me, and for the plainness with which you have stated your intentions. I shall tell you mine with equal plainness."

"I shall be deeply interested in hearing them," said the admiral, with chilling irony.

"I am going to appeal to Admiral Stanton, of the American fleet, for protection."

"I am sorry to tell you that you are too late. Admiral Stanton is a most charming gentleman, but his extreme politeness has led to his return to his native land."

"He has gone home ?"

"Exactly—at the urgent request of the paternal government at Washington. Admiral Stanton is a sailor, and when he meets another admiral afloat, he salutes. He saluted my flag when he entered this harbor, and the Government at Washington, fearing to offend the powerful potentate whom I have shut up in yonder city like a rat in a trap, invited him to return to the bosom of his family."

"Then, sir, I shall appeal to the senior officer of our fleet."

"Captain Picking, of the *Charleston*," said the admiral, with a smile; "another charming gentleman, who will do nothing whatever for you."

"How do you know that ?"

"The Americans, I am told, play a game of cards called 'poker,' in which it is considered clever to try to alarm your adversary by bluster —bluffing, you call it, is it not ? Yes? The fleet which lies at anchor over there is an example of your American bluff. Those ships will not hurt me."

"Admiral Da Gama, sooner or later my bark is going to a wharf or going to the bottom, and I with her."

" Well, my dear captain, you will find the water quite warm and comfortable, even at a depth of ten fathoms."

The admiral arose, indicating that the interview was at an end. Captain Lockwood bowed very stiffly, and, turning on his heel, strode out of the cabin. He marched over the side and down the ladder, and dropped into the stern-sheets of his boat, now alongside, with a sort of emphatic thud.

" Shove off, there," he said. " Get your oars overboard, you Scandinavian kings ; no man-o'-war flubdubbery about it, either. Give way together now, heartily, lads. Lift her, lift her."

At that same hour the bronzed young man who had been languishing in the prison up in the hills back of Rio was engaged in cutting away the stone around the top of one of the bars that guarded the window.

" I suppose the geese don't know I'm a Yankee," he muttered, " or they wouldn't leave me alone here with only three iron bars and an eight-foot jump between me and liberty. I'll give them a lesson they'll not forget."

He worked away diligently, and half an hour later easily removed the bar.

" Now," he said, " here goes for better luck."

He was about to squeeze himself out through the opening when the door opened and his jailer entered. With a shout the man dashed forward. The boy sprang back from the window, and seized the iron bar which he had just removed. With all his force he brought it down on the man's head, and the jailer fell senseless. The next minute the boy climbed out on the window-sill, and with a convulsive spring caught the limb of a tree. In a few seconds he descended to the ground.

"Free!" he exclaimed; "free!"

Then he set off through the woods at a run.

CHAPTER XV

THE *Alma's* boat sped easily across the bay towards the *Charleston*. Captain Lockwood's lips were compressed, and there was a blaze in his eyes. If he had been commander of an American man-of-war at that moment there would have been trouble in Rio Harbor. The light boat shot up easily alongside the ladder, and the captain ran up to the deck. As he crossed the side he lifted his cap and said, with emphasis:

"Thank goodness, I am among civilized men!"

The officer of the deck approached with a smile, and said:

"You speak like an American."

"I am one. I am the owner and master of the bark *Alma* from New York, and I have come to ask for protection from the senior officer of the American fleet."

The officer of the deck at once sent word to Captain Picking, who promptly received the sturdy old skipper. Captain Lockwood told his story with seaman-like bluntness, and the commander of the *Charleston* heard him with courtesy.

"I am afraid I cannot do anything for you," said Captain Picking.

Captain Lockwood stared at him in amazement.

"Why, what on earth are you here for?" he exclaimed.

"I am here to protect American interests in this harbor; but I do not believe that I should be protecting them by doing anything that would appear to favor one side or the other."

"But American ships are being fired on by the insurgents. Mine is not the first."

"I am aware of that; but you must not act in such a way as to draw fire. I can only say to you that if you insist upon going to a wharf, you must do it at your own risk. I cannot interfere in the matter."

"Then I am wasting my time here," said Captain Lockwood, rising to go.

"I advise you to do nothing hasty," said Captain Picking, kindly.

"What do you mean?"

"The American fleet will soon be under another commander, Admiral Benham, who is due here in two or three days. He may see some way to aid you which I do not."

"I thank you for the suggestion. I understand you to mean that Admiral Benham may come with later orders from the national government than those you have, and hence may act differently. You needn't say a word, sir. I appreciate the delicacy of your position, and I'm indebted to you for your courtesy."

And with a sailor-like salute Captain Lockwood turned and left the cabin. In a few minutes he was well on his way back to the *Alma*. On his arrival there, a few words sufficed to put Minnie and Mr. Ball in possession of the facts.

"Well, I'm blowed!" was Mr. Ball's comment.

"You will not try to go to a wharf?" asked Minnie.

"Not till I find out what this new admiral has got to say. But I'm going to shift our anchorage a bit."

The next morning the *Alma* was got under way to stand a little closer under the shore. As soon as her head fell off and her jib filled, a heavy rifle volley was loosed at her from the *Trojano*. The bark was at once brought to the wind and the anchor let go; but even after that several shots were fired across her deck. Captain Lockwood was in deep anger, but he made no further attempt to move his bark. Two days later Admiral Benham's flag was hoisted on the

San Francisco, and a new feeling was aroused in
the fleet of American merchantmen.   Captain
Lockwood waited until another day had passed,
and then he ordered his boat and started for the
flag-ship.   He was a man of stern purpose, and
he had made up his mind that if the American
commander did not promise him protection he
would send Minnie to some place of safety, and
endeavor to run the *Alma* to a wharf in spite of
the insurgent rifles.   Fortunately for him he did
not have to resort to such a hazardous experi-
ment.   He was received by Admiral Benham
with the greatest courtesy, and again told his
story, with the addition of the *Trajano* incident.

"The United States flag," he said, "was flying
aboard my bark the whole time."

"Captain Lockwood," said the admiral, gravely, "return to your vessel. I shall at once enter
into communication on this subject with Admiral
Da Gama, and I assure you, sir, that you shall receive protection from the United States forces
under my command."

Captain Lockwood looked the dignified old
veteran in the eye, and saw there an expression
of quiet resolution which gave him the greatest
satisfaction.

"Thank you, sir, heartily. Good-morning," he
said.

Captain Lockwood went back to the *Alma* and told what had happened. Even Kibo, the cook, was interested, and he set up a barbarian shout of joy that filled the forecastle with discordant echoes. An hour later a launch with an officer seated in the stern was seen to leave the *San Francisco's* side, and hurry away towards the *Libertade*. The officer carried a letter from Admiral Benham to Admiral Da Gama. It was properly a confidential communication, but its contents were soon known among the officers of the American fleet.

"Do you know what it said?" asked George. "It went this way: 'Your right to establish a blockade of the whole or any part of the harbor of Rio de Janeiro is not conceded, and no such blockade will be respected, as belligerent rights have not been accorded you.'"

"W'ich the same it are werry fat talk," said Peter Morris.

"Look here, Peter," said Hal, "you must keep this business to yourself. It will not do to have the men chattering."

"Bless ye, sir," said Peter, "I'll be as dumb as my aunt Mehitabel's big clock wot never spoke but oncet a year, an' then it struck one at one o'clock in the mornin' on the fust o' Janiwary, sir."

"Yes," continued George, who was greatly excited, "and Admiral Da Gama replied that the firing of his ships was not an act of aggression against the American flag, but simply a warning to merchant ships to keep out of the line of fire. He said the shots were always without ball."

"An' that are wot I calls a twister," said Peter.

"Twister!" exclaimed George. "It's a regular—"

"Not so loud, Geordie," said Hal. "It certainly is not true, for Captain Lockwood told us he heard bullets, and one of them went through a sail."

"Are that true?" asked Peter.

"Yes, certainly," said Harold.

"Then afore we leaves this 'ere harbor the American eagle are got to let out one scream, sure."

"Now mind you don't go talking about this among the men," said Hal.

"Among the wot, sir? Slobs, sir—slobs are wot I calls 'em; an' I wouldn't tell 'em nothin' if I thought they was a-bustin' fur to know."

CHAPTER XVI

THE MEETING OF THE CAPTAINS

THE next day the two boys had more news about the correspondence between the two admirals.

"Do you know what Admiral Benham's latest is?" asked Hal, joining George in the steerage.

"No; what?"

"He has demanded that all firing be stopped."

This was true. On January 27th Admiral Benham wrote once more to Admiral Da Gama. "I now demand," he said, "that any order which any ship or shore battery under your command may now have to stop or in any way interfere with the movements of any American vessels about the harbor, while in the pursuit of their lawful business, be rescinded at once. I also request to be notified when this has been done. This demand is not intended to restrict or hamper in any way the prosecution of your military or naval operations." Harold was not acquainted with the wording of this letter, but he knew something about the nature of its contents. The two boys were just going on deck for the second dog-watch, and had paused under the break of the forecastle, where Peter Morris was leaning against the bulkhead.

"Werry good, too," remarked the honest coxswain. "If all the firin' stops, the revolution are over, an' we ups killick an' goes home."

"But do you suppose that Admiral Benham means that Admiral Da Gama mustn't fire at all?" said Hal.

"In course," answered Peter; "ain't that wot he says?"

"No," said George; "only that he mustn't fire on American vessels."

"An' a werry proper order," said Peter, emphatically.

"But," said Hal, thoughtfully, "suppose that Da Gama refuses to comply with this demand?"

"Then I reckon as how we are got to make him," answered Peter. "Else what are we here for?"

"I tell you," exclaimed George, "that would suit me to a T."

"Why Georgie!" said Hal.

"Oh, you needn't look so shocked," said George. "I should like to see some active service."

"So should I," answered Harold, "but in other

circumstances. I can't help thinking of poor Frank's terrible position in this matter. He must be suffering intense agony of mind."

" Hal, I'm just as sorry for Frank as you are; but if there's going to be a row here, I'm going to put him out of my mind and enjoy the fun, and you'd better do the same."

"You let Mr. King alone, sir," said Peter; " when the time comes fur a scrimmage, he'll be right on deck."

" Time's up!" said Harold, shortly. " We must go on duty."

It was a beautiful, clear evening, but warm. A very light breeze was blowing, and the flags on the vessels fluttered rather languidly. George had hardly taken two turns across the deck when he heard a hail from Harold.

"Signals flying on the flag-ship, sir!"

Mr. Harniss, who was officer of the deck, hurried to the bridge, and, with signal-book in hand, noted the flags at the *San Francisco's* signal-yard. The uppermost flag was solid red, the second solid blue, and the third consisted of two horizontal red stripes with a white stripe between them.

"It's 137," he said, turning over the leaves of the book and reading: " ' Commanding officers of ships report aboard flag-ship.' Quartermaster, run up the answering pennant. Orderly!"

The marine who answered the last hail was
sent to inform Commander Brownson of the nature of the signal. Before he had fairly turned
away, Mr. Harniss, anticipating the command
which he knew would come from the captain,
ordered the steam-launch to be got ready and
brought to the starboard gangway, and sent a
messenger after Harold's sword, for it was the
boy's duty to act as boat officer. The crew of
the steam-launch tumbled on deck, and the men
were speedily but carefully inspected by Harold,
to make sure that they were properly uniformed.
The launch had hardly reached the foot of the
starboard accommodation-ladder before Commander Brownson came out of his cabin. A
minute later he was in the boat and on his way
to the *San Francisco*. He spoke not a word
during the brief passage, but kept his eyes fixed
with an expression of deep thought on the vessels of the insurgents, sullenly tugging at their
cables off Engenha. Three other launches, from
the *New York*, *Newark*, and *Charleston*, were
tearing the blue water into ribbons of emerald
and silver as they plunged forward towards the
flag-ship. It looked like a mad race to see which
would arrive first; but as they neared the ship

8

the others slackened speed, and permitted the launch of the senior officer, Captain Picking, to go to the ladder first. The marine sentry at the gangway presented arms, the boatswain's whistle shrieked a shrill salute, and the captain disappeared behind the ship's iron bulwarks. The other officers followed in their order, and in a few seconds Harold found himself sitting idly in the launch, which was bobbing uneasily on the small ripple a few yards off the ship's quarter. There was an air of deep expectancy aboard the *San Francisco*. Though it was a dog-watch, when much latitude is allowed to Jack, the men forward were very quiet. For the most part they sat or lay along the forecastle smoking, and conversing in low tones, with their rough, hairy faces screwed into a hundred queer shapes around the blackened stems of their glowing pipes. Occasionally a louder word or a hoarse laugh rolled over the side, where it seemed to fall into the water and be drowned, so suddenly was it followed by a deeper silence. Even as Nature sometimes appears to brood before she bursts into a storm, so now the flag-ship of the American fleet seemed to be instinct with serious purpose.

In the cabin of Admiral Benham the captains of his ships were listening to a grave communication. The admiral explained to them with great care the exact details of the situation, and gave each explicit orders as to his duties for the following day. These orders caused every man's lips to close a little more tightly, while his eyes sparkled with a new light. Admiral Da Gama had paid no attention to Admiral Benham's letter demanding orders for the final cessation of all firing upon American ships. Now the American commander had finished letter writing, and was preparing to speak another language. The meeting lasted over an hour. Then the launches were called in their order, and in a few minutes Commander Brownson was steaming back towards the *Detroit*. There was a very stern expression on his countenance, and his eyes burned with an intense fire. He gazed steadily at his own ship, and seemed to be making a mental note of every detail of her rig and armament. Then he turned his eyes upon the rebel ships *Guanabara* and *Trajano*, and a grim smile passed over his face. The next moment his eyes met those of Harold, who was watching him with a sort of respectful curiosity.

"Young gentleman," said the commander, in a low tone, "are you much given to cowardice?"

Harold started with surprise.

" I don't know, sir," he answered, modestly. " I have never been tried."

Once again Commander Brownson looked first at the *Detroit* and then at the insurgent ships watching the *Alma*, and he said :

" You may possibly get an opportunity tomorrow to show—"

His speech was cut short by the report of a gun over in the direction of the city. A cloud of bluish-white smoke floating above an insurgent tug told whence the shot had been fired. The tug was about a quarter of a mile above the *Alma*, and to Commander Brownson and Harold she appeared to have fired on that bark. Such, however, was not the case. Under cover of the gathering dusk a young man with reddish-brown hair had stolen out of the woods a mile south of the city, and walked rapidly to the beach. There he took the first boat he saw, shoved off, and began to row up the bay with nervous energy. After he had passed Cobras Island it was evident that he was heading towards the American bark *Alma*. He pulled more slowly now, as if his strength were almost spent. Suddenly a tug steamed out from behind the island. A rough voice bawled an order to the rower to pause, but he redoubled his efforts. The next moment a flash shot out from

"'HELP! HELP!' HE CRIED."

the side of the tug; there was a crash; the forward end of the row-boat was demolished, and the boy found himself in the ill-smelling water. He struggled feebly, for he was almost exhausted.

"Help! help!" he cried, and for a few seconds he disappeared beneath the water.

A boat was lowered from the *Alma* and pulled rapidly towards him. But the tug reached the spot first, and the boy was hauled aboard unconscious.

"Hold on there!" shouted Captain Lockwood, who was in command of the *Alma's* boat; "that man's an American or an Englishman, or he wouldn't have cried 'Help!'"

"He's safe here," was the answer, as the tug began to move away.

"But I want to see him."

"You can't do it. We know this man, and we're going to keep him."

The tug hurried away at full speed, while Captain Lockwood sat in his boat and looked helplessly after it.

CHAPTER XVII

"CLEAR SHIP FOR ACTION!"

THE dull, regular pulsing of the engine of the *Detroit's* launch was all that was heard for several minutes, while the distance between the little craft and the ship rapidly diminished.

"Mr. King," said the captain, suddenly.

"Yes, sir," answered Harold, respectfully.

"What I said to you a moment ago was intended only for the ears of an officer. You understand, sir?"

"Yes, sir; I shall be silent."

"Quite right. You are young in the service, and you cannot learn too soon that between-decks gossip is idle and injurious to discipline."

"Aye, aye, sir," said Harold, rightly construing a suggestion from his commanding officer as an order.

A hundred eyes, filled with expressions of curiosity, were fixed on the launch as she ran alongside the ship. Grave-looking old "waisters" peered out of the broadside ports, their hardy faces showing brick-red beside the dusky bronze

of the shapely 4-inch guns. Lively forecastle
Jacks leaned in unconscious grace over the rails
and studied the captain's countenance. The
officer of the deck stood on the starboard side
of the poop, with the faint crimson light of the
western sky flaming along the edge of his polished visor, and silently watched his superior
mount the ladder, followed by the young cadet.
Harold stood by for orders on reaching the deck,
expecting to be told to see the launch secured
for the night at the port boom, where she had
been allowed to lie.

"Mr. King," said Commander Brownson, lifting his head suddenly as if breaking out of a
reverie.

"Aye, aye, sir."

"Get the launch alongside and lower away
her falls."

"Aye, aye, sir," replied the boy, moving away
to execute the order. It was now nearly eight
bells, when it would be his watch below; but
orders must be obeyed. The captain paused a
moment before his cabin door, and sent a keen
look aloft and along the deck. A shadow of a
smile passed over his bronzed face as he turned
and said to the orderly:

"Present my compliments to the executive officer, and say I wish to see him in my cabin."

The orderly saluted and moved away. A pale yellow glare of electric light flashed and faded as Commander Brownson passed through the door to his cabin. It was growing dark between-decks, though the twilight was still fair enough to make all things visible without. Eight bells were struck, and the interior of the ship rumbled with the tread of feet as the watch below tumbled up to relieve the watch on deck. The forecastle lads stretched themselves and yawned, as they rolled below ready to turn to for a good-night pull at their pipes. Evening quarters were over long ago, and hammocks had been piped down, so Jacky had only to comfort himself till he was ordered to turn in. The sailor is an easy fellow, and he learns to take things as they come. So when the captain returned from the meeting aboard the flag-ship and gave no special orders, Jacky dismissed the incident from his mind.

George Briscomb, as midshipman of the quarter-deck, had been at the gangway when the captain came aboard, and had heard his order to Harold. So, as soon as he was relieved, George asked permission to go and assist Harold. He discovered the launch lying below her davits with her falls hooked on; so he swung himself over the rail, slid down the after-fall, and landed in the boat beside his astonished friend.

" Why, Georgie, what are you after?" asked Hal.

" I just want to have a little talk with you in a place where we can be by ourselves."

The engineer of the launch was busily engaged drawing his fire, and the cockswain and two other hands were forward. Yet, as a matter of precaution, the two boys leaned over the stern with their faces towards the water.

" Now, George, heave ahead," said Harold.

" Don't talk salt, old man," replied George, with a smile; " it's not natural to you."

" I'll talk like a Maine farmer if it 'll please you, George; but what do you want?"

" Did you find out what the meeting was for?"

" No; how could I do that?"

" I didn't know but the old man might have dropped you a hint."

" My dear George, do you suppose that our venerable commanding officer, to whom you refer, with the irreverence of the merchant service, as the old man, has suddenly formed a resolution to take steerage officers into his confidence?"

" Now, Hal, don't sit on me. You know I don't mean anything of that sort. Didn't he let slip any remark that signified anything?"

" Yes," said Harold, slowly, " he did."

"What was it?"

"I can't tell you; he cautioned me to keep my counsel."

"But surely you won't keep it from me?"

"I must, George. You wouldn't respect me if I didn't."

George knew in his heart that this was true; but it did seem hard to him that his friend should know more about the secrets of the fleet than he did.

"I suppose you're right, Hal," he said, mournfully.

"Oh, I say, don't be so sad, Georgie," said Hal, smiling. "Perhaps his words didn't mean so very much, you know."

"Well, I don't believe that meeting aboard the flag-ship was held just to talk about the weather. My! but I can't help feeling excited inside. I'm sure—"

His words were cut short by the sudden burst upon the air of a long, shrill piping from several whistles at once. The two boys sprang to their feet and looked intently at one another as they waited to hear what words would follow. The whistles ceased, and a sonorous bass voice cried:

"All-l-l hands, clear ship for action!"

CHAPTER XVIII

WAS IT ONLY A DRILL?

"GRACIOUS!" exclaimed George. "That means business!"

"Don't stop to talk," said Harold. "Let's get to our stations."

"And I must get my sword."

In a few moments the two boys were aboard the ship, properly accoutred, and at their posts. When the order is given to clear ship for action the officers and crew assemble in the parts of the ship to which they are assigned by the general station bill. As the boys clambered aboard they heard the whole interior of the steel hull resounding with the rapid tread of feet, and though absolute silence is required at such times, it would have been strange if Jacky had not muttered a few complaints about a "bloomin' moonlight picnic when I ort to be doin' forty winks in my hammock." But the discipline of the crew was too good to permit such remarks to be made loudly, and as a rule the men sprang to their stations with alacrity. As the boys hastened to

their places they noted that Commander Brownson and Mr. Crane, the executive officer, were on
the bridge, the former with his watch in his
hand.

"Going to see how long it takes to do the
trick," thought George.

The men attached to the navigator's division
were as busy as bees. Indeed, all hands were
hard at it. In the first place, the steam-launch
and two other boats that were in the water had
to be hoisted up. The sharp piping of the boatswain's whistle urged the men at the falls to put
their strength into their work, and with much
rattling and groaning of blocks the boats rose to
their places, where they had to be secured by the
gripes and with extra lashings, as if the *Detroit*
were bound to sea.

"In with those boat booms," said the boatswain.

Some jumped to let go the forward guys, others
to haul away on the after-braces, and others to
attend to the topping lift-tackle. The lively fellows stationed in the tops sprang aloft with the
activity of cats. Those in the foretop speedily
rigged a couple of quarter-lifts on the signal-yard,
so that it should not fall down on deck and injure
some one if it were shot away. Then the same
hands set to work to sling the fore-gaff in extra

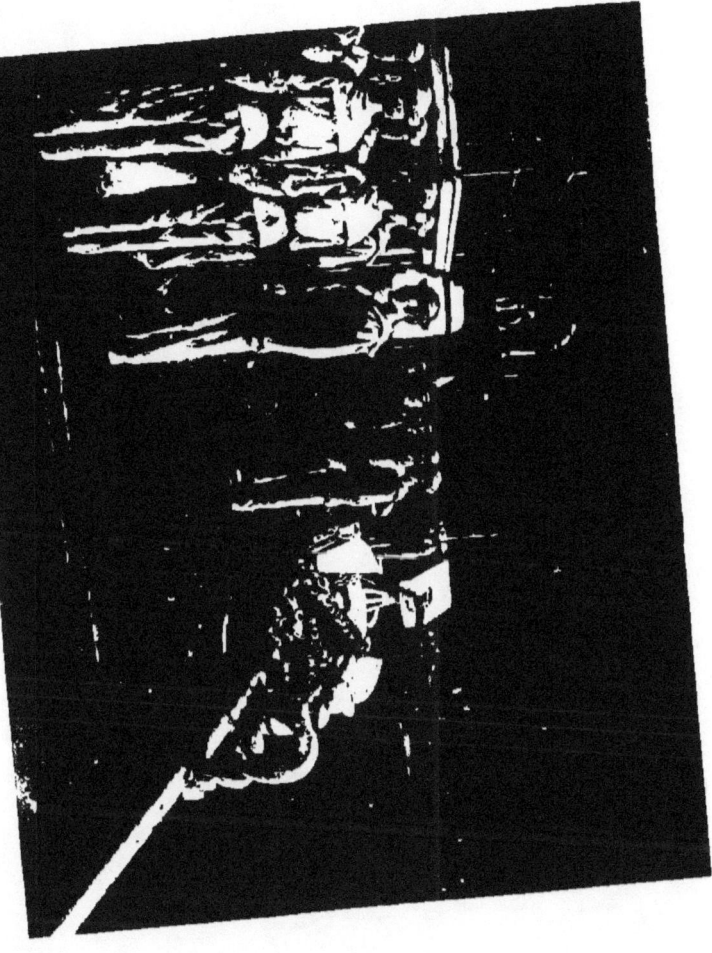

"WAS IT ONLY A DRILL?"

chains with the same object in view. The main-gaff was similarly supported.

"Now, then, shake a leg there," said Harold, who was assisting the officer of the forecastle. "Clear away all that spare stuff."

The willing tars jumped about with celerity at their work.

"Mr. King," said the officer of the forecastle.

"Aye, aye, sir."

"Give special attention to the ground-tackle, and see all in perfect order."

"Aye, aye, sir," answered the boy.

"Don't forget to get the fish-davit out of the way."

"No, sir."

Every nook and corner had to be cleared of odd articles lying about loose, for such things would prove to be in the way when the time for fighting came. Of course the men aboard the *Detroit* were not dreaming of fighting. It is no uncommon thing for a captain to turn his crew out, call them to quarters, load and fire the battery, even at sea, in the middle of the night. In fact, he is required to do this at stated periods to test the efficiency of his crew. This is what the men of the *Detroit* supposed was about to happen, though some of them suspected that there was something beneath all this, and none of them could see just how the firing part of the drill could be accomplished in the harbor.

"I s'pose it 'll be up 'killick' an' git to sea in the mid-watch," said one old growler.

"Werry good," answered the philosophical Peter; "if them's the orders, we ups it an' we gits."

"But wot's the use?" continued the grumbler.

"Mos'ly fur to see," answered Peter, "whether it are the ossifers or the men wot's a-runnin' this 'ere ship."

"Wal, I think it's all nonsense."

"Keep quiet there, and mind your eye," said George, who had just come up.

"Bloomin' young popinjay," muttered the man, under his breath.

The quarter-deck awning had been taken down, and George was having it carefully rolled around the steam-launch, the purpose being to prevent splinters flying, in case she was hit by a shot. In drills aboard a man-of-war everything is done just as it would be in case of a real action. Awning stanchions were taken down, and also boat davits, where they could be spared, and stowed below. The pumps were rigged ready to do what they could towards keeping the water out of the ship if her side were pierced. A thousand and one things had to be done, it seemed, to re-

move every object that could possibly interfere
with the effective working of the guns, and to
secure everything that might get adrift in the
course of an engagement. The men, however,
had been well drilled, the petty officers knew
their business, and the cadets were intelligent
and thoroughly trained. In a few minutes over
half an hour the *Detroit* had assumed the appearance of a man who has taken off his coat and
rolled up his sleeves. Down in the fire-room
there was considerable work yet going on, for
clearing ship for action embraces getting up
steam, and there had been no fires in the *Detroit's*
furnaces for some time, so that her boilers were
cold. When all on deck and between decks was
reported ready, the commanding officer, accom-
panied by the executive and the navigator, made
a tour of inspection. Little, indeed, was there
that could escape the experienced eye of the veteran Brownson ; but both our young friends won
his silent approval of the thoroughness with
which their work had been done. The commander's gaze was searching and business-like, but he
was too old a lover of the sea not to note the
picturesque features of the scene. The dim light
of the newly risen moon fell in a slanting flood
of yellow through the sparse rigging, and made
a thousand strange and mystic shadows on the

dĕck. It threw into sharp relief the sturdy forms
of the crew as they mustered at their stations in
their white working-suits. It lit up the polished
backs of the guns with half-toned splashes of
light, and twinkled softly along the fife-rails at
the foot of the masts. Not a sound was heard
except the foot-falls of the inspecting officers and
the musical babble of the tide around the ship's
forefoot. The captain and his aids passed below
to see that the magazines and engine-rooms and
other interior parts of the ship had been made
ready according to routine. A considerable time
elapsed, and those on the spar-deck knew that
the inspection was being made most thoroughly.
When the officers returned they paused before the
cabin door and conversed for a few moments in low
tones. Then the executive officer and the navigator saluted as the captain passed into his cabin.

"Pipe down," said Mr. Crane.

The shrill whistle of the boatswain once more
broke the silence, its strident tones this time ordering the ship's company to quit stations and go
below. Once more the decks echoed with the
confused trampling of feet, and all hands except
the anchor-watch tumbled down the hatchways.
Once between decks the members of the crew
commented on the evening's exercises in their
own characteristic ways.

" Blow me fur pickles," said one old shell-back,
"ef that there ain't the fust time I ever seed
clearin' ship done in harbor in the fust watch
jess fur fun."

" Er anny other way, either, ole blow-hard,"
said Peter. " You never seed no ship cleared fur
real action."

" Waal, leastways I'm pertikler glad," said the
first speaker, "that we didn't get no orders to
secure."

" We'll have to do 't in the mornin'-watch,"
said another.

" W'ich the same I don't think," muttered
Peter, under his breath.

All conversation among the bluejackets was
cut short by the mellow notes of the bugle sounding the tattoo. The silence of night settled down
over the ship, and Jacky, accustomed to taking
things as they come, speedily passed into the
happy unconsciousness of a dreamland which was
one wide garden of tobacco-plants watered with
grog. On deck the men in the anchor-watch
continued to discuss the evening's work in low
tones, and the officer of the deck paced up and
down in a thoughtful mood. Our two young
friends were about to turn in, when a messenger entered the room and said that the first
lieutenant would like to see Mr. King on deck.

9

The boy went at once, and Mr. Crane said to him:

" Mr. King, I want you to undertake a rather ticklish job."

" Very good, sir," said Harold, quietly.

" You are to go in a boat unarmed, and reconnoitre the disposition of the rebel fleet. You are to make no resistance if attacked, but are to escape, of course, if you can. What you are to try most earnestly to do is to avoid detection."

" Very good, sir."

" If you wish any assistance, you may have it; but it must be a cadet. Officers can't be spared just now."

" I don't know that I need any help, sir; but I'd like to take Mr. Briscomb with me, and Peter Morris for cockswain."

The request was granted, and in a few minutes the five-oared whale-boat, with muffled oars, was moving silently away from the ship. The night had become cloudy, and was intensely dark. Under Harold's direction the whale-boat proceeded to a point above the anchorage of the insurgent war-ships. The tide was ebbing, and the boy had decided to drift down with it, pulling a stroke only when absolutely necessary. The plan was successful. In deep silence the boat with its eight occupants drifted down among the vessels, and Harold's trained eye noted that every one of them was in readiness for an early move. Yet their lookouts seemed singularly inattentive, for the whale-boat was not discovered. At last they were under the bows of the *Trajano*, and George incautiously remarked :

"This beats the deck!"

Instantly a rough voice shouted something in Portuguese from the forecastle-deck, and a rifle was discharged, the bullet passing through the boat's rail.

"Give 'way!" commanded Harold, in a low, sharp tone.

The tars bent to the oars, and the boat shot out into the bay. But the *Trajano's* lightest-pulling boat was in the water, and as the whale-boat moved off Peter caught sight of dark forms tumbling into her.

"They're after us, sir," he said.

"Pull heartily, lads," said Hal.

"Here they come right astarn," said Peter.

All hands were silent for a few minutes.

"Do they gain?" asked Hal.

"I don't think so, sir," said Peter. "It are so werry dark I can hardly tell; but I reckon we ain't a-gainin' either."

Snap! The bow-oar broke off just above the blade. The other four men pulled all the harder.

"That's no good," said Hal. "Hard a-starboard, Peter."

"Hard a-starboard it is, sir," said the cockswain.

After a dozen strokes had been pulled Harold ordered:

"Oars!"

The men ceased rowing, and at the boy's order all hands huddled in the bottom of the boat. The ruse was successful. The cockswain of the Brazilian boat lost track of them in the darkness, and continued to steer straight ahead.

"They're a-passin'! they're a-passin'!" muttered Peter.

CHAPTER XIX

BREASTWORKS AROUND THE GUNS

An hour later the whale-boat safely reached the *Detroit*, and Harold made his report. Mr. Crane expressed his approval, and complimented the boy on his clever escape.

"Hal," said George, as they were turning in, "I hardly know what to say to you. I came near ruining the whole thing."

"Well, Geordie, if you don't know what to say, don't say a word, and let's go to sleep. We haven't much time."

A few minutes later both boys were in the land of dreams. Harold was the first to awake on the call of the messenger, at ten minutes of four in the morning.

"Turn out, old man!" said Harold, shaking George.

"All right!" exclaimed George, rolling out of his bunk and beginning to tumble into his clothes.

It was clear and still when the boys reported on deck for the morning-watch.

"It's going to be an active watch this morning, young gentlemen," said Mr. Burrell, the officer of the deck; "so keep your weather eyes lifting."

"Aye, aye, sir!" came the regular response.

"George," said Harold, a minute later, as they paused a moment near the main-mast, "look down yonder."

The young cadet turned his gaze in the direction indicated, and slowly but deeply the details of the scene impressed themselves upon his mind, there to remain as long as he lived, the memorial record of his first moving experience in the service of his country's flag. Admiral Da Gama had not replied to the last communication of Admiral Benham, but he had read between its curt lines the challenge of a spirit that would not brook light treatment. The bay swam in the glory of the morning sky, silver-blue, streaked with dull crimson and purple. Not a cat's-paw roughened the polished surface of the great natural basin, which was lambent with the radiant reflection of the heavens. The gray slopes of the Organ Mountains formed a strong background for the picture. In the foreground the troubled city of Rio de Janeiro, with its taller buildings lined in sombre silhouette against the sky, seemed to rest in temporary, dreamless

peace. Before the water-front, less than half a
mile from the shore, lay Captain Lockwood's
bark, the *Alma*, swinging to her arched cable,
her yards stripped and squared, and her jib-boom
housed. A slender vane fluttering at her main-
truck, fanned by some gentle upper current that
did not touch the sleeping water, was the only
visible sign of life aboard her.

Just beyond her lay the rebel war-ships *Trajano*, *Guanabara*, and *Libertade*, the latter outside and farthest to the north. Their decks
were silent, not a figure showing above the bulwarks. Slim night-pennants trembled aloft, but
thin, steady streams of smoke flowed from their
smoke-stacks, showing that there were fires in
the furnaces and steam in the boilers. Beyond
these ships, farther out in the bay, lay the *Tamandare* and the massive hull and frowning turrets of the formidable *Aquidaban*. These two
ships were riding to short cables, and both had
steam up. Frank Lockwood was striding up and
down the *Aquidaban's* quarter-deck. His face
was deathly pale, and there were blue hollows
under his eyes. He was suffering the greatest
agony of mind that had ever come into his young
life, for he feared that a general engagement between the insurgents and the American fleet was
imminent. He had determined that he must do

his duty, but the fierce desire of his heart almost amounted to a prayer that the first fire of an American gun might stretch him on the deck.

"This is my punishment," he murmured, half aloud. "I might have known that my wild craving for adventure would bring its own retribution. But would I have suffered any remorse if I had not been brought face to face with the possibility of fighting against my own countrymen? No, no; this is a lesson for me."

Fortunately for Frank, he could not know what an important part his classmates were to take in the approaching scene, or he would have been in still deeper pain. They were at their early morning duties aboard the *Detroit*, and their thoughts were not of Frank at that moment. Harold had mounted the forecastle-deck, where he had a clearer view of the bay. He caught George's eye, and nodded to him to look out again through the port. As he did so he caught sight of a tug well known to be in the employ of the insurgents. She was steaming out from the shore of Cobras Island. She ran along the line of American ships, and it was easy to see that her people were taking accurate note of the condition of preparation aboard each vessel. Having completed her tour of observation, she hurried away with half an acre of foam under her bows and went alongside the *Libertade.*

"Aha!" said Harold to himself, " she is carrying the news to his highness."

"Mr. Briscomb," said Mr. Burrell, at this moment, "send for the bugler."

George was surprised at the order, for it was half an hour earlier than the usual time for getting the bugler ready to sound the reveille; but of course he answered with the ever ready "Aye, aye, sir!" and obeyed at once. It was just 4.30 o'clock when the brisk notes of "I can't get 'em up" rang out on the berth-deck, followed by the shrill piping of the whistle of the boatswain's mate, and the familiar cry : " Turn out all hands! Up all hammocks!" But the routine order was destined not to be obeyed that morning. Before the bugle had ceased to sound, the executive officer, Mr. Crane, swung himself on deck with his cap jammed well down over his eyes.

"Good-morning, Mr. Burrell," he said ; "have you issued the order about the hammocks yet?"

"No, sir," was the answer. "I thought it would prevent confusion to wait till the men began to come on deck."

"Very good," said Mr. Crane. "I'll attend to it myself."

Mr. Burrell saluted and turned away. Mr. Crane mounted the bridge. George, who had heard the brief dialogue, waited anxiously to see what was coming next. His suspense was short. The petty officers and men came tumbling up the hatchways and lined themselves along the rails ready to pass up their hammocks to the stowers.

"Keep fast with those hammocks!" was Mr. Crane's curt order.

Then he called Harold and George, and in a few words told them what he wished. The astonished crew was set to work building breastworks with the hammocks. One was made across the poop abaft the 6-inch rifle, and others around the wheel and across the ends of the bridge. As the men started at this unaccustomed task, a low, irresistible murmur ran along the deck, and for a moment threatened to grow into a cheer. The men looked into one another's faces with blazing eyes and fast-coming breath.

"S'help me, bloomin' bully!" muttered Peter Morris, beginning to look eager, "but it means fight!"

"Cool and steady's the word, lad," said Harold, quietly.

The cockswain looked the boy straight in the eye, nodded his head approvingly, and said:

"Cool an' stiddy, you says, sir, an' cool an' stiddy it is."

The work of building the barricades occupied most of the crew for three-quarters of an hour. Then Mr. Crane gave orders to lower the four boats at the quarter-davits and moor them off the ship. By the time this had been done and the men were back on deck, Commander Brownson came from his cabin and mounted the bridge. At the same instant Harold, whose eyes were quicker than those of the quartermaster on watch, touched his cap and said:

"Signal from the flag-ship, sir."

"Two-forty-nine—get under way," said Mr. Crane.

The next moment the order to weigh anchor was given aboard the *Detroit*, and at the same second George and Harold saw that all the other American war-ships were under way.

CHAPTER XX

" Foul anchor, sir."

That was Harold's report as the anchor rose
into sight, and consequently the *Detroit* advanced
at a very slow pace while the work of clearing
the anchor was in progress. She was moving
straight down the bay, and the other ships of
the American fleet were turning over their propellers just enough to make steerage way. Now
another string of flags rose to the *San Francisco's*
signal yard-arm, and a moment later the answering pennants were flying on the *New York*,
Newark, and *Charleston*, but not on the *Detroit*.
Harold looked wonderingly at the commander
and his aids on the bridge; but it was evident
that they had noted the signal. Harold was
puzzled for a moment, but suddenly he said to
himself :

" We got our orders at the meeting last night."

Commander Brownson picked up a binocular
and took a look at the insurgent ships *Guanabara*,
Trajano, and *Libertade*.

" Our friends over there," he said, laying down the glass, "are preparing to receive us."

He smiled as he spoke, and then curtly ordered the man at the wheel to port a little. The *Detroit's* head swung slowly around till it pointed towards the centre of the opening between Enchadas and Cobras islands, when the order was given to go ahead steadily. By this time it had begun to dawn upon all hands that the *Detroit* had special duty to perform, and there was an air of breathless expectation all through the ship. At 6.25 the bugler was again summoned, and at 6.29 this brisk call was sounded:

" General quarters!" exclaimed Harold, as he sent post-haste for his sword.

" This here are a-gettin' to look like fun," said Peter.

In a moment the ship was alive with a great bustle of action. The men of the navigator's division set to work to rig the hand steering-gear in case the steam-gear should be disabled by shot. They also brought axes and hatchets for clearing away incumbrances on the deck. A spare compass was placed in a safe spot, leads and lines were laid near the foot of the fore-shrouds, and hammock and boom cloths were stopped down. Chronometers and other instruments of navigation had to be stowed away out of the reach of shot or the influence of the jar of heavy gun-fire. Fire-buckets were put in order, the cables extra stoppered and made ready for running, and extra lashings put on the anchors.

The surgeon opened up his case of instruments, and made ready his operating-table in the sick-bay. Basins, towels, lint, bandages, and all the dread paraphernalia of the hospital stood in ghostly array in the white-walled apartment; while the bay-men bustled about, adding here and there a touch to the preparations. Tackles and slings were rigged to lower away the wounded, and the grave-faced surgeon sat, with his coat off and his sleeves rolled up, waiting.

In the powder division, charged with the all-important business of distributing ammunition, activity was at fever-heat, yet everything was done coolly and in order. The officer in command of the division gave the keys of the magazine and fixed-ammunition rooms to the gunner, who distributed them among his mates. The men allotted to the magazines put on their

" GENERAL QUARTERS !"

felt-soled shoes and magazine clothes, and carried wet swabs and cans of water for drinking or drowning fire to their places. The screens were let down, scuttles opened, chutes placed, and shell-whips rigged to hoist the heavy shot to the spar-deck. Hose was uncoiled and led out, and the steam-pump made ready, and watertight bulkheads closed. When all was complete, and the scuttle-men, runner-boys, and whippers at their proper stations, the officer in command of the division reported to the executive officer.

On the spar-deck the guns' crews, under the watchful eyes of the division officers, prepared the big weapons to do their deadly work. The gun captains of the 6-inch guns threw open the breeches, inspected the bores, looked to the gas-checks, put in place the breech-sights, and saw that the necessary appliances were at hand. Other men freed the elevating-gears, placed the loading-trays under the breeches, laid the rammers and sponges on the deck, brought tubs of water and put them at the rear of the guns, and provided cutlasses, revolvers, rifles, and bayonets for the crews. At the 4-inch rapid-fire guns similar preparations, though of a simpler nature, were going on. At the Hotchkiss 6-pounders the crews of four men rapidly made the pieces ready for loading. In the tops men were hoisting ammunition for the guns aloft. The marine guard, with rifles at an order, mustered on the poop-deck, ready to be sent where their services would do the most good. As each division completed its preparations the officer in charge of it reported to the first lieutenant. Little more than three minutes elapsed before the entire battery was ready for loading. Commander Brownson smiled slightly and nodded at Mr. Crane, who gave the order:

"Sponge! Service charge, common shell."

"Werry good, too," murmured Peter; "makes the bore slick."

This order applied only to the 6-inch guns. The big bristle sponges were dipped into the tubs, and then run through the chambers of the guns. The shell-men and powder-men went to the ammunition-scuttles and received the powder and shells from the men at the whips.

"Load!" said Mr. Crane, in a low, sharp tone that was audible all over the ship.

The shell-men of the 6-inch guns entered their shells, which were pushed home by the loaders, the powder following in a similar manner.

"W'ich the same it goes in at the back door werry quiet," muttered Peter, "but comes out o' the front werry lively."

" Peter," said Harold, trying to look stern, but with smiling eyes, "you *must* keep quiet."

The second captains closed the breeches, and the first captains inserted primers, hooked the lanyards, full cocked the locks, and stepped back. At each rapid-fire 4-inch gun No. 4 of its crew stepped up with the cartridge resting in the hollow of his right arm, and shoved it into the breech, which No. 3 closed with a snap. The Hotchkiss 6-pounders and the machine-guns aloft were also loaded, and for a few seconds nothing was heard save the clanking of breech-plugs as the guns were closed. And now every division officer and gun-captain stood gazing intently on the executive officer, whose calm and immovable countenance was as inexpressive as the face of the Sphinx. Commander Brownson stood leaning lightly against the rail on the starboard wing of the bridge. He knew that his ship was ready for action, and he was watching through his glass the movements of the bark *Alma* and the insurgent war-ships. It was evident that Captain Lockwood was aware of the progress of events, and was preparing to make an attempt to move his vessel. It was equally plain that the crews of the *Guanabara* and *Trajano* had gone to quarters. In the momentary breathing-spell that now came, Harold and

10

George had time to look about them. Harold was on the forecastle-deck beside the 6-inch gun, which was under his immediate charge, and George was posted between the two forward 4-inch guns. The *Detroit* was steaming ahead at a four-knot gait, the ripples parting gracefully around her moderate ram bow, and streaming away sternward in glistening ribbons. The sunlight danced on the polished curves of her brasswork, and laid splashes of silver on the chocolate chases of her loaded guns. An intense silence reigned. The officers on the bridge, with swords and revolvers at their hips, stood like statues. The men on the deck were motionless, every dark, eager face turned towards the bridge. A dead calm prevailed in the bay, and it seemed as if Nature herself was astonished at the unwonted spectacle of an American man-of-war prepared to fight.

Bang!

Every man started as the report of a gun rang out.

"Now what's coming?" Harold asked himself, as he listened for the shrieking of a shell.

"'Taint fur us, sir," said Peter, in a low tone. "It are a small pup of a rebel tug up yonder."

"Here they come; I wonder what they're up to?"

At that moment Commander Brownson had the *Detroit's* engines stopped, and gave the crew orders to stand at ease. He was entirely too wary to be drawn into the local quarrel.

"Them small fry is exchangin' of compliments with the shore batteries," remarked Peter.

"I wonder what our own ships are doing?" said Harold.

"They ain't a-loafin', sir," said Peter. "Look, sir. There's the *'Frisco* a-lookin' out fur the batteries on Cobras an' Enchadas islands."

"Yes, and here's the *Charleston* a mile astern of us. She must be our support."

"An' look at the *Newark*, sir, a-layin' broadside to broadside with the *Tamandare*."

"And the *New York* is laid opposite the *Aquidaban*," said Harold. "That will be the centre of the fight."

"Lord bless ye, sir," said Peter, "it 'll never git as fur as that. If we kicks 'em oncet they'll squeal an' run."

"And, Peter, does it occur to you who's to give the first kick?"

"W'y, we is; an' bully well we'll do 't, too, sir."

And then that one big, significant thought seemed to flash upon the minds of all the *Detroit's* men. The little gunboat had been honored with the task of making the initial move-

ment.   She was to voice Uncle Sam's imperative
demand for justice to his merchant ships and
respect for the stars and stripes.   Every man
turned a hungry gaze on the *Guanabara*, *Trajano*, and *Libertade*, and the gun-captains fingered
their lanyards.

The insurgent tugs, barking like mongrel curs,
swung in wide curves away from the shore, and
circled out among the merchantmen.   A few
scattered, sullen shots, and they steamed slowly
away.   Commander Brownson swept the bay
with his binoculars, pausing for a more careful
survey of the *Alma*.   He hung the glass on the
bridge rail, placed himself beside the engine-room
telegraph, and signalled :

"Ahead slowly."

The propellers began to revolve, and the gunboat advanced.   Harold noted that the shore
was black with people, and that the roofs of the
houses in the city were crowded with persons
eager to see what the despised Yankees were
about to do.

"Port," commanded Captain Brownson.

The helmsman obeyed the order, and steadily
the *Detroit* swung round, heading so as to pass between the bark *Alma* and the insurgent war-ship
Trajano.

CHAPTER XXI

THE SHOT ACROSS THE BOW

Up the bay the decks and rigging of the foreign war-ships were crowded with men gazing at the unwonted spectacle. It must have presented features for especial consideration to the senior captain of the English fleet, for he had already refused to do for a British merchant captain what Admiral Benham was now doing for Captain Lockwood. As for our two young friends, they were strung to an intense pitch of excitement, for they fully believed that they were about to go into action. George, nervous and active, could not stand still, though he was far from feeling as much apprehension as Harold. The latter saw that the *Detroit's* situation, exposed to the fire of three ships at once, was highly dangerous. But the boy was as steady and cool as a veteran, and as he stood near the breech of the big 6-inch rifle, with his hand lightly resting on the butt of his revolver, Peter Morris, who was captain of the gun, could not repress many nods of approval. An involuntary gesture by one of the men called

the attention of all hands forward to the movements of the *Alma's* crew. The monotonous,
metallic clank of her capstan-pawl told that her
cable was slowly coming in, and presently the
stock of the anchor appeared, parting the lucent
water under her fore-foot. Now a boat, which
had been lying under her port bow, started forward. In it were four seamen and Mr. Ball, the
mate. They were engaged in an attempt to run
a warp from the *Alma* to the vessel ahead of her,
by which to haul her in towards the shore. Mr.
Ball stood up in the stern and hailed the *Detroit.*

"Are we to understand that you're here to see
us through?"

"That's our intention," replied Commander
Brownson. "You go ahead and take your boat
to the wharf."

"That's what we're a-doing," replied Mr. Ball;
"but we're afraid they'll fire on us."

"I don't think so," said Commander Brownson, quietly. "But you must risk that."

Captain Lockwood, standing on the poop of
the *Alma*, saw Harold, and waved his hand at
the boy, at the same time calling to his mate:

"Go ahead there, Mr. Ball; the tide 'll be drifting us off shore in a minute."

"Give way, lads!" exclaimed Mr. Ball.

The four sailors bent their backs to the oars,

and the boat, dragging the line, began to move slowly ahead.

"Ready with that forward 6-pounder," said Captain Brownson, in a low tone.

"All ready, sir," answered the division officer, calmly.

The eyes of the captain of the gun sparkled with excitement as he eagerly waited for the order to fire. But it was not Commander Brownson's intention to become the aggressor.

"Keep steady there, my lad," he said, quietly.

"Look!" exclaimed Harold, involuntarily, yet under his breath.

The men of his crew heard him, and gazed in the direction indicated. They saw a marine on the poop of the *Trajano* slowly raise his rifle, take deliberate aim at the *Alma's* boat, and fire. The sharp crack of his weapon rang across the water, and Mr. Ball, rising in the boat, shook his fist at the insurgent war-ship. At the same instant Commander Brownson spoke in a stern, suppressed voice:

"Let her have it, lad, just abaft the stem, betwixt wind and water."

Bang!

A great fountain of white smoke spurted from the 6-pounder rapid-fire gun mounted on the starboard rail of the *Detroit*, abaft the break of the forecastle. But from some unaccountable cause the gun-captain had misunderstood the commander's plain order, heard by every one else, and the 6-pound shell plunged into the water about a yard ahead of the *Trajano's* stem, throwing a shower of spray over her forecastle. Immediately Commander Brownson signalled the engine-room to stop the engines, and as the *Detroit* drifted ahead, he said :

" Train all guns on the *Trajano.*"

" Left, ha-a-nd-somely," came the low orders of the gun-captains ; and the trainers swung the breeches of the guns slowly to the left till the yawning muzzles pointed directly at the insurgent ship.

" Steady, lad," said Harold, in a low voice, to Peter, who was holding a taut lock-string.

"Don't worry, sir," was the reply. " I won't pull till I gets orders."

" *Trajano* there !"

Commander Brownson's sharp hail cut the air like a keen sword.

" Aye, aye," came the sullen response.

" If you fire again," called the commander, in a clear, high tone, which must have made every word audible to Admiral Da Gama aboard the *Libertade*, " I will return your fire, and if you persist in firing, I will sink you."

There was not a heart aboard the *Detroit* that did not leap with exultant pride as these brave words rang out, and as for Captain Lockwood, he threw up his cap and emitted a stentorian cheer. The insurgents appeared to be completely amazed. For fully a minute not a movement was made aboard the *Trajano*, though her officers could be seen in anxious consultation. Finally, at the expiration of two minutes, she fired a gun from her port battery, her starboard side being towards the *Detroit*. Such an action is interpreted among men-of-war's men to mean submission. The officers of the *Detroit* smiled contemptuously, and the gun-captains looked disgusted. The little gunboat was forging slowly ahead under her own momentum, and Commander Brownson, again using that ringing tone which made every word audible to the insurgents, hailed the *Alma:*

"Aboard the bark!"

"Aye, aye, sir!" answered Captain Lockwood, with a fine emphasis on the "sir."

"Go ahead to your wharf, if you wish to."

"And if they fire on me?"

"You go ahead; I will protect you."

The crew of the *Alma* cheered, and the four men in the boat with Mr. Ball carried their warp to the ship ahead. The *Detroit's* engines were started again, and she moved forward with only mere steerageway. She was now drawing abreast of the *Guanabara*, and in a moment it was seen that the crew of this insurgent ship was at quarters. The eight Armstrong rifles and the machine-guns had been cast loose, loaded, and trained on the *Detroit*.

"Perhaps now we shall get a broadside," murmured Harold.

"Well, sir," whispered Peter, "we mustn't keep wot isn't ourn, an' so I reckon we'll give it back."

"Train on the *Guanabara*," said Mr. Crane.

The muzzles of the *Detroit's* guns swung slowly so as to bear on the vessel.

"*Guanabara* there!"

It was Commander Brownson's voice once more.

"Tell your men to handle their lock-strings very carefully. See that no shots are fired by accident, for I am not going to regard any as accidental."

No answer was made to these words, and the *Detroit* passed on.

"Port," said Commander Brownson to the man at the wheel.

The helm was put over, and the gunboat turned across the *Guanabara's* stern. Her engines were stopped and reversed, and the vessel lay motionless in a position to rake both the *Guanabara* and the *Trajano* with her starboard battery. But the movement of the tide made it impossible for the gunboat to maintain this position with the limited space she had to work in, so Commander Brownson gave orders to get a buoy-rope on the starboard chain and make ready for letting go the anchor. Harold jumped to help to superintend this work, which belonged, of course, to the forecastle. A few minutes later the *Detroit* came to anchor with all ready for slipping her cable and getting under way at an instant's notice. Perhaps no one was more surprised at the cool audacity of this manœuvre than Admiral Louis Phillipe Saldanha da Gama.

CHAPTER XXII

A SLAP IN THE FACE

As the *Detroit* lay there Harold noticed that several small armed vessels under the command of the insurgent admiral had drawn near, and were hovering within range of the *Detroit*. He decided that the trouble was not yet at an end. And he was right. The *Alma* was still busily engaged in warping in, when a loud report broke upon the air. All hands aboard the *Detroit* started as they saw a cloud of white smoke rising from the *Guanabara's* side, and realized that she had fired one of her broadside guns across the *Alma's* deck. Commander Brownson's brow was black as night as he sternly said:

"Stand by your guns, lads."

Then he spoke a few low and rapid words to a marine, who was standing near him. The man raised his rifle, and, taking deliberate aim, sent a bullet whistling into the *Guanabara's* stern-post. Such an action was like a contemptuous slap in the face, but it contained a threat that the deadly broadside might follow. The *Guanabara* re-

"THE MAN SENT A BULLET WHISTLING INTO THE 'GUANABARA'S' STERN-POST."

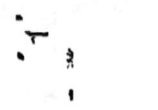

ceived the shot in silence. Commander Brownson watched the insurgent ship quietly for a minute, and then gave orders to lower away a boat. While the execution of this order was in progress, the commander's eyes slowly roamed over the forms of the half-dozen cadets who stood at their posts on deck. His gaze finally rested with an expression of satisfaction on Harold.

"Mr. King," he called, "come up here."

"Aye, aye, sir," replied Harold, starting with surprise.

"You will go in the boat to the *Libertade*," said the captain. "Present my compliments to Admiral Da Gama, and deliver to him this message."

Commander Brownson now spoke rapidly to Harold, whose attitude was one of intense attention. When he had received his orders, the boy saluted and hurried away to the boat, an object of envy to every other cadet aboard the ship. He urged the boat's crew to lively pulling, and was soon alongside the insurgent flag-ship, which was not over two hundred yards away He found Admiral Da Gama on the bridge, surrounded by his staff. The boy saluted respectfully, and said:

"I have the honor to bear a message from Commander Brownson, commanding the United States steamer *Detroit*."

He paused a moment, but no one replied. They stood and glared at him with their sparkling dark eyes. But, as we have already seen, Harold King was a lad of cool and steady nerve.

"Commander Brownson presents his compliments to Admiral Da Gama," continued Harold, in a clear, firm voice, "and says that while he is not desirous of taking any active steps, he has his instructions from the admiral commanding the United States fleet to protect American ships in going to wharves. He desires to say to you that he will carry out those instructions by replying to any shots your vessels may fire; and should you persist in firing, he will open upon your ships with the *Detroit's* entire battery."

Admiral Da Gama's face was pale and his lips twitched, but he answered, steadily:

"You will present my compliments to Commander Brownson, sir, and say to him that should he fire on my ships I shall at once lower my colors and request Admiral Benham to take command of my fleet. The gun fired to leeward by the *Trajano* was a gun of protest, not a challenge."

Harold had some difficulty in concealing his surprise at this remarkable message, but he contrived to preserve the composure of his countenance, saluted, and returned to his boat.

"Give way with a will, lads," he said to his crew.

The rhythmic click of the oars and the washing of the ripples were the only sounds that were audible. A great silence of suspense seemed to hang over the harbor. The brave little *Detroit*, defiantly anchored under the guns of the *Trajano*, *Guanabara*, *Libertade*, and the smaller vessels, made an inspiring foreground to a naval picture whose distance was finely filled by the imposing hulls of the *Aquidaban* and the *New York*. The *Detroit's* boat was watched by every eye in both fleets. Had a single treacherous shot been fired at her from a Brazilian craft a terrible and deadly storm of iron would have followed. Harold sat bolt-upright in the stern-sheets, and did not deign to cast a glance at the rebel ships. He mounted swiftly to the *Detroit's* bridge as soon as he reached her side, and repeated to Commander Brownson the words of Admiral Da Gama. The veteran's lip curled with contempt as he said :

" You will return at once, sir, to the flag-ship of the insurgent fleet. Present my compliments once more to Admiral Da Gama, and tell him that I have already fired on and struck his ships."

Some of the officers on the *Detroit's* bridge turned away to hide the smiles which this message caused. The insurgent admiral must indeed have been blind if he did not see from his own deck the treatment of the *Guanabara*. Harold quickly returned to his boat, and once more shot away towards the *Libertade*. Again he mounted her bridge, and repeated his captain's words to the admiral.

"Sir," said Da Gama, "you will say to your commanding officer that I have already called a conference of my captains, and my advice to them will be to surrender at once to Admiral Benham, and request him to carry on all negotiations with the Brazilian government in regard to our future treatment."

It is hardly necessary to say that when this proposition was subsequently conveyed to Admiral Benham he smiled at it. He had no desire to saddle himself with the settlement of Brazil's family troubles. His mission was to protect American interests, and to stop at that. For the present, however, the message of Admiral Da Gama went no farther than the *Detroit*, where it was correctly repeated to Commander Brownson by Harold. The commander smiled, and said to his executive officer:

"Well, Mr. Crane, I am afraid we shall not have any battery practice here."

Then he turned, and, with a kindly nod, said to Harold:

"Have the boat hoisted, and return to your station, sir."

Harold hastened away to obey, and as he left the foot of the ladder leading to the bridge he passed close to George.

"Lucky boy!" said George, in a low tone. "You were right in it."

Harold returned to his post, where Peter was waiting for him.

"Wot did I tell ye, sir?" said the cockswain. "We kicks an' they squeals. They're reg'lar slobs!"

"What's the *Alma* doing?"

"She's a-gettin' nearer to the wharf."

"Hello! Here come those tugs again."

The two insurgent tugs steamed down close to the *Alma*.

"Keep a sharp eye on those fellows," said Commander Brownson.

One of the tugs steamed around the *Alma*. Suddenly a dishevelled figure burst out of the cabin of the little steamer and sprang upon the rail as if about to jump into the water. A shout arose on the tug, and half a dozen armed men rushed forward and seized the young man, but not before he had uttered one wild cry that flew far across the waters:

"Father!"

11

Captain Lockwood, standing near the knight-heads of his bark, heard the sound, and started as if he had been struck by a shot.

"That was Bob's voice!" he said. "Bob, my boy, where are you?"

An inarticulate and muffled cry was the only answer. Robert Lockwood—for it was indeed he—had been forced back into his temporary prison aboard the tug, and Captain Lockwood began to believe he must have been the victim of a delusion. But Harold King had seen every-thing from the *Detroit's* forecastle-deck.

"It's the captain's son," he said, "and the reb-els have got him again."

"W'ich the same," said Peter, very sagely, "we knows w'ere he are; an' if you an' Mister Bris-comb an' me ain't able fur to git him away, then them Dagos is werry much smarter than their ships."

CHAPTER XXIII

THE " WIG-WAG " SIGNAL

"Now how on earth are we to manage it, that's what I'd like to know," said George.

"Not by being impatient," said Hal. "We must keep cool and think."

"Right, sir," said Peter, who was a party to the council. "As my old mother used to say, fust do a good deal o' thinkin', then a good deal o' talkin', an' then mebbe ye'll be fit to do a little doin'."

"First of all," said Harold, "we must let Captain Lockwood know that we saw his son in the hands of the rebels."

"Werry good," said Peter, "an' then him an' you talks it all over an' shapes a course for wot are to be did next."

"Exactly," said Harold. "But first of all we've got to get permission to go ashore, so that—"

"Mr. King, the first lieutenant wants to see you," said a messenger, coming up.

In a few minutes Harold returned with beaming eyes.

"It's the finest kind of luck," he said, "but I'm ordered to go ashore on an errand. I have permission to take you with me, Geordie, and Peter's to be our cockswain."

" When are we to go?" asked George.

"Right away," answered Hal.

" Werry good, too," said Peter. " I goes an' I gets the boat."

Harold had already reported his orders to the officer of the deck, and in a few minutes the boat was at the starboard gangway. The boys set off for the shore in good spirits, and were not long in finding their way to the *Alma*, where they were heartily welcomed by Captain Lockwood and Minnie.

"That was a great time we had two days ago," said the captain. "But I'll admit that although I came to the wharf I was sorry to see the American ships return to their berths without giving Da Gama a thrashing."

" But you forget Frank!" exclaimed Hal.

" Well, for his sake I'm glad there was no fight."

" We have some news for you," said Hal.

" About Robert?" exclaimed the captain.

"He's in the hands of the rebels," said George.

" Oh, I've learned that," said the captain. " It was Bob that called to me from the tug the other day. But my agent here can't find out where he is now."

"Then they have him hidden somewhere." said Hal.

"That's it; but where?"

"Frank is our man," said Hal, after a moment's thought. "He must get his friend Bennos to find out for him."

"Do you think Bennos will do it?" asked the captain.

"I don't know," replied Hal, "but I see no other way. Anyhow, captain, you work your way, and we'll try to communicate with Frank. Between the two we ought to get something."

The boys now went to attend to their errand, and in a short time were on their way back to the ship. While they had been ashore Frank had heard a piece of news that filled him with the deepest anxiety. The boy had picked up enough of the language to understand a good deal more than the Brazilians thought he did, and he had overheard a conversation which made him intensely anxious to communicate with his uncle. Unfortunately he was allowed no liberty at all, because the Brazilians, knowing him to be an American, had no faith in him now. So Frank now set about contriving some plan by which he could communicate with Harold and George. He knew that whatever he was to do must be done quickly, for the *Aquidaban* might at any moment up anchor and stand out to sea again. But plan as he might he could think of no way to meet his two classmates. It is said that when Fortune is at her worst she turns favorable, and she certainly now favored Frank.

"*Amigo mio*," said Bennos, approaching him as he stood leaning over the taffrail; "some men are to go to the beach to swim. You are to command the boat."

The beach referred to was on Engenha Island, near which the *Aquidaban* was anchored. It was half a mile away from the war-ship, and as pleasant a place for bathing as could be found in such foul waters.

"All right," said Frank. "Are they going right away?"

"*Si, amigo*," replied Bennos.

The boat, with some twenty-five Brazilians in it, was brought alongside, and Frank seated himself in the stern-sheets.

"How long are we allowed?" he called to Bennos as the boat was pushed off.

"Till the next watch begins," was the answer.

That meant nearly two hours. In fifteen

minutes the boat was on the beach and the men
were undressing.   Frank did not feel like swim-
ming in Rio Harbor.

"Take charge of the men," he said to the
principal petty officer.

Then he walked away towards a short, bluff
point, which terminated the beach at one end,
and sat down on a rock.   He was half lost in
moody speculation when he chanced to notice
that he was almost abeam of the *Detroit*.   By
walking around to the side of the point farthest
from the beach, and out of sight from the deck
of the *Aquidaban*, he found himself directly opposite the American gunboat.

"Now," he thought, "if I could only signal
the boys.   But of course it wouldn't do."

At that moment an American man-of-war's
boat came around the end of the island nearest
the city.   There were two officers in the stern,
but it was impossible to identify them at the
distance.   However, as the boat advanced it
drew nearer to the island, and Frank began to
fancy that he recognized one of the officers as
George.

"They'll be past in a few minutes and out of
sight around the other point," he muttered.   "I'll
risk it."

He broke a short, straight branch off a bush and

tied his handkerchief to it, making a small but distinct signal flag. Then selecting a place where the light was good, and there was a solid background of green, he began making the three motions to the left which represent the letter D in the navy wig-wag code. D is the "call" letter of the *Detroit*. He made the signal half a dozen times in vain, and he thought the boat was about to pass out of sight around the end of the point, when suddenly the men ceased rowing. One of the officers in the stern took off his cap, and, without standing up, waved it twice to the left, twice to the left again, and then once down in front of him. That meant that the signal of Frank was seen and understood.

"Jolly good thing I know my wig-wag so well," thought Frank; "and if those beastly Brazilians should see these signals they couldn't read them."

Frank now rapidly wig-wagged this message:

"Frank Lockwood would like to say something to Hal King or George Briscomb."

"We are both in this boat. Will come ashore," was the answer.

"Pull in diagonally; don't let men bathing see you land," signalled Frank.

The hint was taken, and five minutes later

"HE MADE THE SIGNAL HALF A DOZEN TIMES IN VAIN."

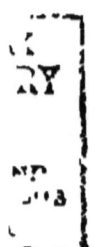

the light whale-boat was scraping her keel on the sand behind the point.

"It's lucky we were sent off on an errand just when you were ashore," said George, grasping Frank's hand.

"We've been to see your uncle," said Hal.

"Is he well? And Minnie?" asked Frank.

"Both are well. We had news for them," said Hal.

"We've seen Robert," blurted out George.

"Where?" demanded Frank.

Hal rapidly told all that was known about the unfortunate son of the captain.

"That still further complicates matters," said Frank.

The anxious, strained look in the boy's face made Harold grave at once.

"There's something serious, isn't there?" he asked.

"Yes," said Frank.

"Then let's hear it right away."

"Come over here."

The three boys went and sat down on a rock, and Frank opened the story of his troubles.

CHAPTER XXIV

A COWARDLY PLOT

"I suppose," he said, "I needn't tell you fellows that I wasn't particularly happy when you cleared for action the other day."

"No, Frank," said Harold; "we thought about you."

"I'm sure you did," said Frank.

"But," exclaimed George, "it must have been a little consolation to you to know that none of our class are aboard the *New York*."

"But there are cadets there," declared Frank; "Watkins and Glenn and Carver—fellows we knew well at the Academy. Do you think I'd have felt like starting a 70-pound shell in their direction?"

"No, of course not," said Harold, warmly. "George, don't speak so hastily."

"Besides," continued Frank, with great emotion, "do you think I couldn't see the flag at her taffrail? A fellow doesn't feel much like turning against the flag which four years of his life have taught him to reverence."

The three boys were silent for a few moments, and then Frank continued:

"But I didn't wig-wag you to come ashore just to tell you what oughtn't to be any news to you."

"No," replied Hal; "but I would like to ask you one question about that affair."

"What is it?"

"What did you intend to do that day?"

Frank paused a few seconds before he answered. with much solemnity:

"Get myself wounded if exposure to fire would do it."

"Oh, I say, old man!" exclaimed George, in a shocked tone.

"You'd have done the same thing if you'd been in my place," said Frank, earnestly.

"But fortunately for us all," said Harold, soothingly, "nothing came of the demonstration."

"No," replied Frank; "the kind of fighting that our admiral saw in your admiral's eye was something we're not accustomed to down here."

Again the three were silent for a few seconds, and then Frank said:

"As soon as the thing was over and we had returned to our anchorage I went straight to the old man and asked leave to resign from the service."

"And what did he say?" asked George.

"He laughed at me," answered Frank. "He refused to listen to any such proposition. I tried to make him understand my feelings, but he was inflexible. He said that there could not by any possibility be any further collision between us and the United States fleet. I told him I was sick of the whole business anyhow, but he said that was no reason at all. Others were sick of it, too; but he had never known any service in which there was not discontent. He met all further argument on my part by a cold declaration that he would not accept my resignation, and that any attempt at desertion would be treated according to the usages of war."

"The old brute!" exclaimed George.

"I answered that I had no idea of deserting; that I felt myself in honor bound, as he would not release me, to serve my time out."

"There doesn't seem to be any help for it," said Harold, sympathetically.

"But he has no faith in my honor," said Frank.

"What makes you think so?" asked Hal.

"I can see that I am watched most of the time," responded Frank; "and they don't allow

me to get out of sight. This trip ashore was
permitted only because they know I'm with a
boatload of men, and they don't think I can escape from the island."

"But Bennos?" queried Hal.

"Oh, I think he understands me," answered
Frank; "he does not think I would desert."

"I'm glad of that," said George; "I took quite a
fancy to that fellow. And we may need his help."

"How?" said Frank.

"Never mind that now," said Hal. "Tell me
first why the *Aquidaban* is likely to go out at
any time."

"There is a report that the government cruiser
Nictheroy has been seen not far up the coast,
and that she is coming down here. We intend
to meet and engage her outside."

"My!" exclaimed George; "then there will
be a big fight."

"Yes," said Frank; "but she has not made
her appearance yet. Nevertheless, we are likely
to up anchor and go out at any moment. And
that's why I consider myself so lucky to catch
you to-day. I don't know how I should ever
have managed to communicate with you, and
you were my only hope."

"Your only hope, Frank? What do you
mean?" asked Hal.

"It is of vital importance that I get a message to my uncle, Captain Lockwood," said Frank.

"Too bad you didn't catch us when we were going ashore," said George.

"Yes, we could have delivered it, of course," added Hal.

"My uncle must be warned somehow to keep his weather eye lifting, because they're brewing trouble for him."

"Who?"

"Our people—the insurgents. I overheard a conversation aboard the *Aquidaban* this morning."

"What was it?"

"I know a heap more about their lingo now than they think I do," said Frank, "or they would have been more careful. What I made out was that there's a scheme afoot to scuttle the *Alma* at her wharf to-morrow night."

Harold and George looked horrified.

"To scuttle her?" exclaimed Hal.

"Why, Frank," declared George, "that's not warfare; that's rank piracy."

"It's a piece of contemptible cowardice," said Frank, hotly; "but it's worthy of the rebels. Mind you, it's not to be done by any of the people in the fleet. They're a deal too careful of their precious hides to venture ashore. It's to be done by some agent of theirs in the city."

"Then we must not lose any time," said George, rising.

"Wait a moment," said Hal. "Peter, come up here."

The cockswain left the boat and approached the cadets. Hal repeated Frank's story to him.

"Do you think we could get permission to go ashore again to warn Captain Lockwood?"

"Waal, sir, I should say as how we could, cos w'y, we're here to pertect American interests, an' if them isn't they, wot are?"

"Good; we'll try it. Meantime this is what we need of Bennos," said Hal, speaking rapidly and decidedly. "He must find out for you where Bob is, and you must tell us."

"Suppose he doesn't know."

"Then you can't help us. Anyhow, the bark must be saved first," said Hal.

"How am I to get word to you?" asked Frank.

"Beggin' your pardon, sir," said Peter, "an' I kin give a plan."

"Go ahead."

"Write yer news an' put it into a bottle. Werry good. W'en you sees our boat a-leavin'

the ship you chucks the bottle overboard, an' it
drifts down to where we picks it up, sir."

"That might work," said Frank.

"We must try it," said Hal.

The friends now separated, the cadets hastening back to the *Detroit*. They had no serious
difficulty in obtaining permission to go ashore
again to warn Captain Lockwood. But they
looked in vain for the bottle which Frank was
to throw overboard. If they had reflected, they
would have known that they had not given him
time enough to accomplish his purpose. Filled
with disappointment, they made the best of their
way to the *Alma*. To their dismay they learned
that Captain Lockwood and his daughter were
ashore. So were the mates.

"Here's a go," said Hal. "No use telling the
sailors."

"We might leave a note," said George.

"No," said Hal; "you know Captain Lockwood would only laugh at it, and think we were
easily frightened."

"Then we must wait till to-morrow," said
George. "The plot is not to be put into execution till to-morrow night, you know."

"And in the meantime we may hear from
Frank," said Hal.

They returned to their boat and started back

to the *Detroit*. When they were at a point directly to the southward of the *Aquidaban's* anchorage, Peter suddenly cried:

"There she blows! I mean there she floats—the bottle, sir."

In another minute they were alongside of it and had it aboard.

"My cousin," said Frank's note, "is said to be confined in the house of a rebel sympathizer named Miguel Santos, on the great northern road, four miles beyond the city. I enclose chart of the location. But my informant is not sure that he is there. He is condemned to be shot."

"We must get off for the whole day to-morrow morning, and search for the boy first," said Hal.

CHAPTER XXV

THE CADETS TO THE RESCUE

As soon as the boys reached the *Detroit*, Harold went to Mr. Crane and told him the whole story.

"Now, sir," said the cadet, "I hope you'll allow Briscomb and me twenty-four hours ashore to warn Captain Lockwood and to help him find his son. And I'd like very much to have Cockswain Morris to go with us."

"I must talk to the captain about this," was the reply.

Commander Brownson at once perceived that it was a matter of which official notice could not be taken without more definite information; yet to wait for that might mean destruction to the *Alma*. He gave the desired permission, and the executive officer ordered a boat to be in readiness to take the three friends ashore immediately after quarters the next morning. It was understood that they were to return to the *Detroit* in one of the *Alma's* boats in twenty-four hours. As soon as they reached the landing-place they

went at once to the *Alma*. Captain Lockwood
was greatly agitated by the news which they
gave him.

"So they want to shoot my boy and razee the
bark, eh?" he exclaimed. "Well, by the great
horn spoon! I guess we'll beat them at both
games. But I can't see why they've put Bob
ashore. I should think they'd have kept him
aboard one of their ships."

"Beggin' yer pardon, sir," said Peter, "but
seein' as how he are a American, they wants to
keep their doin's dark."

"That must be it. But we haven't any time
to lose. We have to get horses yet."

"And the bark?" asked Hal.

"Oh, Mr. Ball can take care of her. He'll take
her out of the wharf and anchor her."

"But it would be better to defer doing that
till late in the day, so that they may not have
time to form a new plan," said Harold.

"That's so, boy; you have a clear head."

"And as we shall probably get back after
dark, we ought to know where she's going to
be," continued Hal.

"Right again. You're a sailor, sure."

"W'ich the same he are, sir, beggin' his pardon
fur sayin' so," said the cockswain.

The first mate was sent for and let into the

secret, but he was instructed not to tell the crew.

"Now, Mr. Ball," said Captain Lockwood, "about four o'clock or later you stand by to get the bark off. Anchor about just off Encha-das Island, bearing no'-no'theast from the wharf, say about three-quarters of a mile."

These instructions having been given the captain arose to go, but Harold said:

"One minute, sir. It will not do for us to go on this expedition in uniform. Can't you fit us out with some old toggery from your slop chest?"

"Right," said the captain.

"And to make everything snug and safe," said George, "I think we ought to shift somewhere ashore."

"There's a friend of mine who lives right on the outskirts of the city," said the captain, "and we can have our horses sent there, and shift there, too."

The party, consisting of the captain, the two cadets, and the cockswain, now arose to depart. The first mate was instructed to have a boat at the landing-float at eight o'clock to wait for them.

"Good-bye, all," said Minnie. "I wish I were a man so that I could go with you."

They set off with grave faces, the cockswain carrying the bundle of clothes to be used as disguises. Captain Lockwood was well acquainted with the city, and he knew where to procure horses. It was decided that they should get the animals at once and ride out to the house of the captain's friend. An extra horse for Robert was to be sent after them. On arriving at their destination Señor Pereira, the friend of Captain Lockwood and a loyal Brazilian, heard their story, and said that he was ready to give them every assistance. He knew the house of Miguel Santos, and suggested that they should all ride out in that direction in the afternoon and reconnoitre. As soon, therefore, as they had eaten, they mounted their horses and set off. In spite of the gravity of the occasion George could not help laughing.

"Señor Pereira," he said, "did you ever see anything more absurd than four sailors on horseback?"

The polite Brazilian made some courteous remark, but Peter shook his head, and said:

"Werry bad, werry bad; but not no wuss nor a sea-sick sojer aboard ship, w'ich the same he are 'most as distressin' a sight as a cat in swimmin'."

The four miles were soon covered, and Señor Pereira pointed out the house. Captain Lock-

wood was very excited, and the boys had much
difficulty in calming him. Suddenly, as they
walked their horses slowly past the place, Harold
exclaimed, in a suppressed voice:

" I see him!"

Captain Lockwood looked in the direction indicated, and there was his son in an upper room.

" There are no bars to the window," said
George; " why doesn't he escape?"

"He must be fastened in some way," said Hal.

" Nothing but chains would hold him," said
the captain.

"Then we must bring a steel saw to-night,"
said Hal.

" Have you thought of a way to reach him?"
asked George.

" W'ich the same I have did," said Peter, significantly.

" Did he see us?" asked the captain.

" No," said Hal; " but we ought to let him
know that we are around."

They turned back and rode past the house
again. Captain Lockwood began to whistle a
peculiar tune. Robert heard it, raised his head,
and saw his father, who at once laid his finger
on his lips, and rode on. They now returned to
Señor Pereira's. The Brazilian sent a servant
to purchase a steel saw, and now there was noth-

ing to do but wait for darkness. As soon as it was dusk the rescuers set off, Peter having provided himself with a large coil of rope. When they arrived at a point about two hundred yards away from the Santos house, they led their horses into the woods and made them fast. Then they stole on foot to the rear of the house.

"Georgie," whispered Harold, "here's your chance. You used to be fond of playing Indian scout. Now see if you can find out where the people of the house are."

George needed no second bidding. Pulling off his shoes, he threw himself on his breast in the thick grass and crawled away. He was gone more than half an hour and his friends became very anxious, when suddenly he reappeared.

"It's all right," he said. "The family is just going to bed; they are evidently early risers. There are two men with rifles in a front room on the first floor, but they have a table with a bottle of wine and cards on it. They'll be too interested to watch their prisoner."

They waited about three-quarters of an hour longer, and then Peter was directed to go ahead with his scheme. The seaman at once climbed a tall tree at one side of the house, carrying an end of his rope up with him. Harold followed him. A long branch of this tree extended nearly over the roof, and climbing out on it, Peter, with a sailor's dexterity, cast the bight of the rope around a chimney. He now made the ends fast to the tree limb. Then taking another piece about thirty feet long he slung it around his body, and by means of his extemporized bridge, he crossed hand over hand to the roof, Harold following him. The piece of rope which Peter took over was made fast immediately above the window where Robert had been seen, and then Peter descended by it to the window-sill. The window was latched. Peter laughed quietly, and taking out his knife inserted it between the two sashes and freed the latch. He stepped into the room, which was pitch dark.

"Who's that?" called a voice.

"Are you Robert Lockwood?" asked the cockswain.

"Yes."

"We're here fur to save you. Come with me."

"I've got chains on my ankles."

Peter examined them and found them too heavy to saw through in a short time. So he made the end of his rope fast around the boy's body and climbed back to the roof, where he

"THE CAPTAIN SAW HIS SON DESCENDING."

and Harold, with much labor, hauled the boy out through the window until he hung suspended in the air. A moment later the captain saw his son descending to the ground. He started forward quickly, and the next instant the boy was clasped in his father's arms. As soon as Peter and Harold had descended, they lifted Robert and carried him to his horse in the woods.

"You'll have to ride side-saddle fashion, Bob," said the captain, laughing.

"I can ride that way as well as any other," replied the boy.

Their progress was slow, but in three-quarters of an hour they were at Señor Pereira's. There a cold chisel was obtained, and, not being afraid to make a noise, the chains were cut from Robert's ankles. The horses were left at the house of the Brazilian, to be returned in the morning; the cadets and Peter put on their uniforms, and, with many expressions of gratitude to Señor Pereira, the party set off at a brisk walk for the wharf. Minnie and Mr. Ball had rowed the dingy ashore themselves, and were waiting for the party. Just as Captain Lockwood set his foot on the inshore end of the wharf a splutter of dampness broke against his face.

"What's that?" he exclaimed. "Fog, as I'm a living man."

"It 'll be a werry bad job to find your bark, sir," said Peter. "Cos w'y? huntin' fur a wessel in a fog are like huntin' fur whales in Broadway, New York."

CHAPTER XXVI

LOST IN THE FOG

IT was difficult even to find the landing-float, so dense was the oily blackness which the fog spread over the whole shore and bay.

"It are werry much like lookin' down the neck o' a bottle o' ink," muttered Peter.

But presently Mr. Ball heard their footsteps, and in a low voice called out:

"Is that you, cap'n?"

"All right," answered the skipper; "here we are."

The next minute they were in the boat, and Minnie, half crying, had her arms around her brother's neck. Mr. Ball, Peter, and the two cadets took the oars.

"Wait a bit," said the captain; "let's get our bearings. You anchored just where I told you, Ball?"

"Yes, sir, but I'm sorry—"

"Sorry for what?"

"I couldn't find a boat compass to bring ashore."

"Goodness!" exclaimed the captain, "there are three aboard, but they're all in the locker in my cabin."

"Well, sir," said Peter, after a moment of silence, "I reckon we got to feel fur her."

"We'll be mighty lucky if we find her," said Hal.

"Yes, but we can't stay here," said George.

"Couldn't we wait till the fog lifts?" asked Hal.

"These fogs in Rio Harbor generally hang on all night," replied Captain Lockwood. "If it wasn't for Minnie we might lie right here till daylight."

"Oh, papa, please, please don't think about me," said the girl; "think about saving Robert."

"An' beggin' your pardon once again, sir," said Peter, "if we stays here till daylight, an' the fog lifts, doesn't we stand a good chance fur to be seed by some o' them rebel tugs afore we git off to the bark?"

"Why, of course, cocks'n," said the captain. "You've got your wits about you. We must do the best we can to find the *Alma*. Let's see, now. This wharf here runs about due north and south. We must get our bearings as well as we can from that. Give 'way, lads."

The four oars dipped into the water and the

boat started. The landing-float was instantaneously hidden from sight, and the boat appeared to be floating in darkness.

"It's a mean, dirty night," said the captain.

"I am not in love with it," said George.

"It has one advantage," said Harold.

"What's that?" asked the captain.

"If we can't find the *Alma*, they can't either."

"True enough," answered the captain; "but I don't think they would undertake to harm her while she's out in the bay."

"We must be pretty nearly there," said George.

"Oh no," said Mr. Ball; "we haven't pulled three hundred yards yet, and she's a good three-quarters of a mile out."

They rowed on for several minutes in silence. Then they ceased pulling, and listened.

"I don't hear a sound," said the captain. "I think we might try a hail now."

"Very well, sir," said Harold.

"*Alma* ahoy!" shouted the captain.

They all waited, but there was no reply.

"We're not far enough out to be heard in this fog," said Hal; "let's pull ahead."

For a few minutes nothing was heard save the monotonous click of the oars in the rowlocks.

"I think we'd better try it again," said the captain.

He lifted up his voice and shouted the name of the bark once more, but again there was no reply.

"Young gentlemen," said the captain, "I'm afraid we've missed her."

All hands were silent for a moment. They knew too much about the water to question the judgment of an experienced mariner like Captain Lockwood.

"Don't you think, sir," said Hal, "that we must try to find her?"

"Of course," said the captain. "But if we do find her it'll be because we stumble on her by chance."

"I'm mortally sorry about this," said Mr. Ball.

"It's not your fault, Ball; you've done the best that could be done in the circumstances."

"Why, we can steer by the wind!" exclaimed George. "I remember distinctly how it was blowing when we started out."

"Oh, Georgie, Georgie," said Harold, with comic dismay; "that's a dreadful break for a fellow who was brought up on the sea-coast."

"Why, I'd like to know—"

"A wind, sir," said Peter, "are like a young

woman's mind, beggin' your pardon, miss. It changes w'en ye don't know it are a-movin' at all."

George was silent, and presently they began to row again. Even while they had been lying on their oars the boat's head had swung about three points unknown to them, and they were now pulling down the bay. They were already half a mile below Isla de Cobras, though they thought themselves half-way across to Nictheroy. Presently they paused, and the captain again shouted :

"*Alma* ahoy !"

But there was no answer.

" We must row on," said the captain ; " that's our only chance."

The four oarsmen bent their backs to the oars again. For nearly two hours they pulled in every direction, as they imagined, but in reality in a zigzag course down the bay. At the end of that time they were outside of the bay and in the cove just behind Sugar Loaf Mountain, though they believed themselves to be up near Engenha Island.

" There's no use of killing ourselves," said the captain. " We're in for a night in the streets, and we may as well let her drift."

A moment later Harold said :

" Listen ! I hear water lapping against a rock or a ship."

" Look !" said George, "there's something; it's a vessel."

A dark mass loomed above them in the fog, and the boat drifted against the side of the ship.

" Whoever she is," said Captain Lockwood, " she'll not refuse us shelter. On deck, there !"

" Wait, wait !" cried Harold, who had placed his hand against the vessel's side and discovered that it was iron.

It was too late, however. Lights flashed along the ship's rail, and a voice hailed them in Spanish.

" Speak ' English,' " said Captain Lockwood.

" In the boat there," called a firm young voice ; " come aboard and surrender yourselves."

They had no choice but to obey the order, and climbing aboard, they found themselves face to face with Frank Lockwood.

" Uncle Hiram! Bob !" he exclaimed.

" It seems we're your prisoners, Frank," said Robert, bitterly.

" An' all that horseback ridin' fur nothin'," muttered Peter.

CHAPTER XXVII

HAROLD USES STRONG WORDS

"I suppose we're aboard the *Aquidaban*," said Captain Lockwood, after a few moments of silence.

"That is true," said Frank; "though for the life of me I can't understand how you came here."

"Lost in the fog, my boy, trying to get aboard the *Alma*."

"Then she has left her wharf?"

"Yes, she's safe at anchor."

"And you've all been ashore to rescue Bob?"

"That's it."

"But, Uncle Hiram, this is simply terrible. He's under sentence of death, and here the whole lot of you have walked straight into the lion's jaws."

"It seems that I am doomed to bad luck," exclaimed Robert. "I'd better end it all now; there's plenty of water here."

He made a movement towards the ship's rail, but Harold and George seized him.

13

"Wait a bit, sir," said Peter; "never sink so long as ye can swim, an' there ain't no hole knocked into ye yet."

"My son," said Captain Lockwood, gravely, "there must be a way out of this. Be patient."

"Bob, old fellow," said Frank, "I've suffered enough since I was such a fool as to enlist under a foreign flag. Don't add to my misery. We must find a way to save you. Do you know where you are?"

"Never a bit, except that we're on Mello's deck," answered the captain.

"You're in the cove just south of the Sugar Loaf."

"Great Scott!" exclaimed Hal; "we must have rowed over four miles trying to find the bark."

"But now that we're here," said Captain Lockwood, "what's to be done with us?"

"I don't know," said Frank; "I haven't made any report yet. I was ordered to find out who you were and what you were about. If you'll just wait here till I report, I'll soon be able to let you know."

Frank hastened away and laid the case before the officer of the deck, who fortunately chanced to be his good friend Roderigo Bennos.

"You must tell the captain," said Bennos.

Accordingly he directed Frank to carry the

report in person to the commanding officer. The boy did as he was ordered, but he did not deem it necessary to say that the American skipper who had come aboard was the captain of the bark *Alma.*

"Let them remain," said the commanding officer.

"But if they should wish to go ashore when the fog lifts?"

"Let them remain till I am ready to talk to them."

Frank saluted and left the cabin. He understood that, although nothing of the kind had been directly said, the *Alma's* party were prisoners. The boy was hot with indignation, but he had no tangible fact to grasp, and even if he had he would not have profited by expostulation.

"You are to remain aboard the ship for the present," he said, when he had rejoined his friends.

"And Bob?" demanded the captain.

"Well," said Frank, "perhaps no one will recognize him, and you may be able to get him off when you go."

"But," said Hal, "if they should afterwards discover who he was, Frank, you would be in serious trouble for letting him go."

"I'll take my chances of that," said Frank, decisively.

"God bless you!" said Captain Lockwood, wringing his nephew's hand.

At that moment the shriek of a boatswain's pipe arose. and a command was shouted.

"What's that?" asked George.

"It's up anchor," said Frank. "I suppose we're going up the bay. We came down only last night, but up and down like a seesaw appears to be a large part of our business."

"What's to become of my boat?" asked the captain.

"We'll tow it up," answered Frank.

"I suppose that 'll do," said the captain.

He was by no means satisfied with the aspect of affairs, yet there was nothing that seemed to call for a serious complaint. The monotonous clanking of the heavy cable was now the only sound that disturbed the night. The fog was drifting off in writhing shreds among the crannies of the mountains, and the dim light of a young crescent moon fell across the peaceful waters. Presently the ship began to swing slowly around, showing that the anchor was aweigh. Then the calm of the night was suddenly broken by the blare of a bugle.

"What's that?" asked Hal, with a sudden start.

"That's quarters," said Frank. "We never attempt to go into the bay without going to quarters. As soon as we poke our bow out of the cover of this mountain Fort Santa Cruz will open on us."

"But," said Hal, sternly, "your commander has no right to put us under fire of the fort. Your uncle and cousin are non-combatants, and George and I are officers in the service of a neutral power."

"I know all that, Hal," said Frank. "I'll see Uncle Hiram and Minnie, together with Bob, in a place of safety—though, for the matter of that, almost any place is safe, for they seldom hit us —but I don't see that I can do anything for you."

"Let me see the captain."

Harold's request was taken to the cabin and he was invited to enter. An interpreter had to be provided, and then the boy said:

"We are citizens of the United States placed aboard your vessel by accident. Our boat is towing astern, and we desire to leave your ship."

"It is not convenient for me to stop now," was the reply.

"I protest, sir, against your course as outrageous," said the boy, calmly and firmly.

"Your protest is of no avail," was the answer.

" You have no right to place two American officers and an American seaman under fire," said Harold.

" If the American officers are afraid they are at liberty to go below the water-line," said the Brazilian commander.

" Afraid!" exclaimed Harold. " We come from the *Detroit*."

At these words the Brazilian's face became very stern.

" You will remain aboard this ship," he said, " till we reach our anchorage. We shall then set you ashore ; not before. As for the merchant captain and his children, we shall do as we like with him."

" Very well, sir," said Harold, taking advantage of the officer's mistake ; " I shall make it my business to have this affair reported in detail to Admiral Benham, and if you do the slightest harm to Captain Lockwood or his children you may rely upon it that the commander of the American fleet will blow you out of the water."

With these words the boy turned and strode out of the cabin without saluting.

CHAPTER XXVIII

A SHELL THROUGH THE PORT

THE boy rejoined his party on deck and reported the failure of his mission.

" They're a fine lot," said Captain Lockwood.

At this moment Frank, who had been attending to his duties in preparing the guns for action, returned.

" Come," he said to Captain Lockwood, " you and Minnie and Bob must be put in a place of safety."

" I wouldn't go if it wasn't for her," said the sturdy old seaman.

" Oh, nonsense!" exclaimed George. " You don't want to give these fellows the satisfaction of seeing you hurt, do you? Besides, it may prevent Bob from being recognized."

They all descended to the gun-deck, where Frank paused to point out to them the particular gun which he commanded.

" I don't wonder you're sick of the whole business," said Hal.

Just then the captain of the ship appeared,

and calling Frank to him asked what he was
doing. The boy explained briefly. The Brazilian captain smiled, and said :

" Tell your two young naval friends that I
should be delighted to give them guns to command."

" I wonder what he's talking about?" asked
George, who saw from the man's face that the
words referred to himself and Harold.

Frank went over to the boys and repeated his
superior officer's words.

" The impudent old scoundrel!" exclaimed
George.

" Bully boy!" said Captain Lockwood.

Minnie's face expressed alarm mingled with
admiration for the boy's boldness. The Brazilian commander stepped over to where they were
standing.

" Accept my compliments, sir," said Harold,
looking the Brazilian full in the eye, " and understand that we both command guns which
your friends aboard the *Guanabara* did not care
to hear speak."

The officer's face flushed, and he spoke sharply
to Frank :

" Put those two young men under arrest."

Frank turned pale and stood speechless and
motionless.

" Do you hear my order?" demanded the captain.

"Sir," said Frank, drawing his sword and offering the hilt to his commander, " I cannot obey that order."

The Brazilian stood for an instant regarding the boy with amazement.

" Cannot obey!" he ejaculated.

" No, sir," said Frank; " these gentlemen are my countrymen, my classmates, my friends. It is not—"

" Enough, sir! Do as I bid you, or I will—"

" I don't care what you do!" cried Frank. " I have suffered too much already in the service of a foreign flag. I have tried to resign, but you have refused to let me. Now I wish I could die. But so sure as there is a sun in the heavens, so sure will I refuse now and forever to lift my hand against the American flag or any man who serves it."

The Brazilian drew his revolver and levelled it at the boy. Harold and George both sprang before him, the former seizing his arm.

" Here, arrest these two fellows!" cried the officer to the nearest gun's crew.

" Are you crazy?" asked Harold.

At that instant the heavy roar of a gun from Fort Santa Cruz was heard, and a deafening crash told that a well-aimed shot had struck the *Aquidaban* above the deck. Captain Lockwood threw his arms around his terrified daughter and drew her to his breast. The Brazilian commander with a mighty effort gained control of himself.

"We shall speak of this matter at another time," he said to Frank. "Your friends may remain at liberty. To your station!"

The boy saluted and went to his gun. A petty officer led Captain Lockwood, Robert, and Minnie to a safe place behind the armor belt. Harold and George remained on the gun-deck quietly watching the operations. The leisurely manner of the Brazilians caused the American boys to smile contemptuously.

"No wonder this war lasts so long," said George.

"And no wonder so little is accomplished," added Harold.

For once, however, the soldiers of the republic in the forts seemed to be aroused to activity. The scene became intensely interesting. The powerful battle-ship was weak in propelling force, her engines being in poor order, and she moved through the narrow entrance to the harbor slowly. She was a shining mark in the faint moonlight, and had the soldiers been better shots great damage might have been done to her. She was a noble sight as she thundered up the bay, her sides ablaze with the constant flashing of her mighty guns, and a vast canopy of gray smoke rolling over her. The forts every second sprang into red and glowing relief against the hills as their bellowing guns lit up the night and set the echoes booming along the rocky crests. Occasionally a terrific shock would be felt as a heavy missile struck one of the turrets or the armor-belt of the *Aquidaban;* but, as a rule, the shots passed harmlessly above her decks or plunged into the water, sending tall columns of ghostly spray up into the moonlight.

Frank Lockwood was doing his duty with reckless bitterness. He watched the range, and kept the breech-sight rightly placed with ceaseless vigilance. He was continually running from the breech of his gun to the port and giving directions to the gun-captain. He seemed to be determined that the weapon should do deadly work.

"Stupid!" he exclaimed to the gun-captain; "you pull your lanyard before you have covered your mark. What is the use of wasting ammunition so?"

The man muttered something in Portuguese.

"Any American cadet can shoot better.

George, come and show him how to hit the fort."

"Of course I will!" exclaimed George.

He sprang forward, and was about to take the lanyard from the man's hand when Harold seized his arm.

"What on earth are you thinking about?" cried Hal. "Do you want to be dismissed from the service?"

"Dismissed? Why?" asked George, pausing.

"For firing on a friendly fort."

"But it is not I who fire," said George; "it's the *Aquidaban*."

"Nonsense!" exclaimed Harold.

"It's good sense, I think," declared George.

"No, old man, you're wrong."

"Well, the skipper 'll never know anything about it."

"You can't be sure of that."

"You would tell?"

"No; but such things can't be kept secret. Some of these men would talk about it, and it would eventually become known."

"Come, come!" cried the division officer. "Why is that gun silent?"

Frank stepped forward and took the lanyard from George's hand.

"Harold is right," he said. "I am the only

"HAROLD SPRANG FORWARD WITH A LOUD CRY."

American naval cadet who has a right to do this
—I, Frank Lockwood, the mercenary."

The boy bent down and glanced along the
sights, giving orders to the trainers and elevators
in a firm tone. Suddenly he jerked the lanyard,
and the gun roared out its message. At almost
the same instant there was a deafening report,
a blinding glare, and a great cloud of dust and
smoke. A small shell from the fort had entered
the port and exploded against the gun-carriage,
shattering it and dismounting the gun. For a
few seconds no one could see what had happened. A moment later the smoke cleared away,
and it was discovered that one man lay stretched
upon the deck. Harold sprang forward with a
loud cry :

"It's Frank !"

In an agony of fear and grief Harold and George bent over their classmate, and sought to ascertain the nature of his injury.

"Oh, Frank!" exclaimed George; "can't you speak?"

"He's unconscious," said Harold. "He ought to be removed to the sick-bay."

"These fellows don't seem to know what to do," said George, impatiently.

"I wish Bennos were here," Harold said.

One of the sailors seemed to catch the boy's meaning.

"Bennos!" he ejaculated. "*Si, si*, Bennos."

The man hastened away. At the same moment the firing ceased. The *Aquidaban* had passed out of accurate range of the forts and was opposite the city. The bugles sounded the order to secure, and presently the guns were put to rest for the night. Bennos came running along the deck while the bugles were still sounding.

"*Oh, amigo mio!*" he cried, sorrowfully, as he saw Frank's unconscious form.

He speedily gave orders for the removal of the boy to the sick-bay. He was evidently indignant that so many precious minutes had been wasted.

"Perhaps he'll bleed to death; no one will care," said the young Brazilian, angrily.

A stretcher was brought and Frank was placed on it. Two stalwart seamen carried him to the sick-bay, where the ship's surgeon at once began to undress him preparatory to making an examination. Harold and George stood outside the door of the room in feverish anxiety. They turned their heads at the sound of heavy footsteps, and saw Captain Lockwood, Bob, and Minnie coming towards them. The boys grew a shade paler, and looked at one another anxiously.

"What shall we say to him?" asked Harold.

"Or to her?" said George.

The captain approached with a smile, and said:

"Thought you'd get down out of the line of fire, too? Well, that shows your good sense. You'd be mighty stupid to take chances of getting hurt in a quarrel that don't concern you."

"Oh, the firing's all over now," said George, with an attempt to be cheerful. "Robert ought to keep out of sight, sir."

"Oh, this deck's about deserted. Well, for my part, I'm glad the firing's done; aren't you, Minnie?"

"Oh yes, father; I think it's terrible, and I can't help fancying I see some poor fellow torn by shot."

"Not so very much danger of that in a ship of this sort, is there, boys?"

"No; not so much as in a wooden ship," said George.

"Still," said Harold, gravely, "men do get hurt sometimes in the most powerful battleships."

"I hope no one has been hurt on this ship," said Minnie, with apprehensive eyes.

The boys were silent.

"Some one has been hurt," said the captain.

"I was sure of it from the way you talked," said Minnie.

A faint moan was heard coming from the room behind the boys.

"What's that?" asked the captain, starting.

"What place is this?" inquired Minnie.

"This is the sick-bay," said Harold.

"That's the ship's hospital," explained Captain Lockwood. "But why do you stand in front of the door?"

"We are waiting to know whether our friend

is badly wounded," said Harold, in a trembling voice.

"Your friend? Why, say, it's not that nice young Brazilian officer, is it?"

Again the boys were silent.

"Oh, father!" cried Minnie, "they don't dare to tell us. It's Frank!"

The stout old merchant captain staggered as if he had received a heavy blow.

"Don't tell me it's the boy!" he said.

Harold grasped the honest mariner's hand.

"I wish to Heaven I could tell you it was not," he said.

For a few moments the captain was speechless, while Minnie cried quietly.

"Are the doctors working over him in there?" Robert finally asked.

"Yes," said George; "and Bennos is helping them. We could do nothing because we don't understand the language."

"How did it happen?" asked the captain.

"Well, sir," said Harold; "Frank was not pleased with the marksmanship of his gun-captain, so he thought he would take a shot himself. He sighted the gun very carefully and fired. Almost at the same instant a small shell from the shore came whizzing through the port and burst on the side of the gun-carriage. It

14

must have struck the forward end of the carriage, I think, and that's what makes me hope that Frank isn't badly hurt. The bulk of the carriage and the breech of the gun must have been between him and the explosion; so I think he was struck by a small fragment. Anyhow, when the smoke cleared away we saw him lying on the deck."

" Unconscious ?"

"Yes, sir; I must say that he was."

" How long has he been in the sick - bay ?" asked Robert.

" About ten minutes."

" Then surely they ought to be able to give us some news of his condition," said the captain.

Just then Bennos opened the door of the sick-bay wide enough to speak to the boys.

" The doctor can't tell yet. He must examine a little more," he said.

Bennos retired into the sick-bay, and the four watchers resumed their anxious vigil. The minutes were hours long to them. The captain paced up and down with his hands behind his back and his head bowed. He looked as if he were in deep thought, but ever and anon a heavy sigh told that his heart was full of grief. The girl stood watching him and occasionally wiping away her tears,

which flowed freely. George shifted about rest-
lessly, but Harold stood like a statue, with clinched
lips and strained eyes. Presently the door swung
open and Bennos appeared once more. The four
watchers turned eagerly, and George said :

" What's the verdict ?"

" I am glad," said Bennos, speaking rapidly.
" He is not badly hurt. The most trouble is the
shock and the loss of blood. He will get well
surely, but slowly."

" Thank Heaven !" exclaimed the captain, fer-
vently.

CHAPTER XXX

THE night was a long and weary one for Captain Lockwood, his daughter, and the two boys. Bennos offered to give up his state-room to Minnie, but she naturally declined to pass the night separated from her father. Through the kind offices of the young Brazilian they were provided with cushions and blankets and permitted to sleep on the locker in the mess-room. The two boys and Robert were given hammocks and allowed to swing them in a roomy corner. As they overhauled the clews and cast off the lashings George said, with a faint smile :

"Hal, this takes me back to *Constellation* days. I shouldn't be surprised if we were turned out in the night to reef top-sails."

"I wish there were no possibility of our being turned out for anything more serious," said Harold.

"But you are not alarmed about Frank now, are you ?"

"I hardly know what to think," said Hal ;

"I wish he was in the hands of our own surgeon."

"Then you haven't confidence in these fellows here?"

"Not of the most perfect kind."

"Well," said George, thoughtfully, "they must know their business. It's likely that the best surgeons in the service are aboard this ship."

Harold lay awake for a long time considering what was to be done in the morning. He was unable to solve the problem, especially as he and his two companions had to be aboard the *Detroit* again before ten o'clock. At length, worn out by the events of the day, he fell asleep and slept soundly till reveille. Immediately after breakfast he went to Bennos and informed him of the necessity of returning to the *Detroit*. Captain Lockwood, who was now at Frank's side, was sent for.

"I'll stay here for the present," said the old mariner. "You boys and Mr. Ball get Bob aboard the *Alma*, if it's possible, and then Mr. Ball can send the boat back for me later in the day."

"I don't know just how to manage about Bob," said Hal.

"Beggin' yer pardon ag'in, sir," said Peter, "an' I'd like to make a siggistion."

"Go ahead," said Hal.

"Waal, sir," said the cockswain, "Mr. Robert he are took werry sick, werry sick, indeed; an' we has to cover up his head, sir, fur to keep the sun from him, an' so we carries him down into the boat an' lays him along the bottom, an' there he stays till he are safe."

"Peter," said Hal, "you're a jewel."

The boys now applied, through Bennos, for permission to leave the ship, which the Brazilian commander was pleased to grant. The *Alma's* boat was got alongside by Mr. Ball, and the party prepared to depart.

"Leave me to do all the yarnin'," said Peter; "cos w'y? wot good are a sailor wot can't tell a yarn, egspegially to save a young gemman?"

Peter covered up Robert's head and supported him to the deck as if he were very sick indeed. He was taken to the boat and caused to lie down. Minnie trembled and turned pale with anxiety as the boat pushed off. They had gone safely about fifty yards when Robert raised his head for some reason; a whiff of wind blew the light covering off it and overboard. At the same instant a sailor on the *Aquidaban's* forecastle uttered a loud cry and rushed aft, shouting and pointing at the boat.

"You've been recognized," said Hal. "Pull, lads, pull."

"In the boat there!" came a hail from the *Aquidaban's* deck. "Cease rowing, or we'll fire."

"Pull hard," said Harold, between his set teeth.

Bang! A shell from a rapid-fire gun struck the water not three feet from the boat. Minnie shrieked.

"Hold on," said Robert, springing up. "My sister mustn't be exposed to fire. Take me back and surrender me."

"Wich I reckon that are about all we can do," said Peter.

"Worse luck to it," muttered Mr. Ball.

Slowly the boat returned to the ship's side.

"Come on board, all of you," was the order.

It was obeyed in silence. The Brazilian commander was standing at the gangway.

"So, my fine young American friends," he said, "you are trying to help a condemned deserter to escape."

"Yes, he's condemned, but I dare you to shoot him," said a voice behind the Brazilian.

Turning, the officer found himself confronted by Captain Lockwood, who was glaring at him with blazing eyes.

"Pray, sir, what authority have you in this matter?" demanded the Brazilian.

"Just this," was the reply. "I'm the captain of the American bark *Alma*, which you didn't keep away from a wharf, and which your agent on shore didn't destroy last night; and that young man is my son."

The Brazilian captain stared in amazement. For several moments he hung his head in deep thought. Then he said:

"This matter must be placed before Admiral Da Gama. In the meantime your son must remain a prisoner here."

"And my daughter?"

"She may return with your mate to your ship."

"And what do you intend to do with us?" asked Harold.

"I shall report your conduct in this matter to your commanding officer."

"You needn't trouble yourself," said Harold: "we shall do that ourselves the moment we reach our ship. Our leave expires in three-quarters of an hour."

"Indeed?" said the Brazilian, with a grim smile. "Well, you'll stay here till I can get a boat ready to send you to your ship."

"Why can't we go in Captain Lockwood's boat?" asked George.

"Because it's not my pleasure," was the curt reply, and the officer walked away.

"Waal," said Peter, "as my ole mother remarked when she fell into the bar'l o' vinegar, 'here's a pooty pickle.'"

"Anyhow," said Captain Lockwood. "Minnie and Mr. Ball must go to the *Alma*."

So the mate of the bark slowly pulled the heavy dingy away. It was over half an hour later when a boat was reported alongside to take the three Americans to the *Detroit*.

"The captain hasn't been in any hurry about this," said Harold.

"He has intentionally made us late," declared George.

The oarsmen in the cutter must have had orders to take their time, for they did not break their backs in pulling towards the *Detroit*. It seemed to the two boys that they would never reach her. They were fully one hundred yards away when the bell chimed out the hour of ten.

"Pull, you lazy rascals!" cried George.

"No use now, George," said Hal; "we're late."

The cutter ran alongside the ladder and the two boys leaped to the deck. They found themselves confronted by the executive officer, Mr. Crane.

"What cutter is that?" he asked, sternly.

"The *Aquidaban's*, sir," said George; "we—"

"You come from aboard her?"

"Yes, sir; we were—"

"I didn't ask you where you were or what you were doing. You got permission to go ashore for a specific and proper purpose, and you come off from an insurgent man-of-war after your leave has expired. You are both under arrest."

"Under arrest!" exclaimed both boys.

CHAPTER XXXI

TRYING TO SAVE A LIFE

WHEN the two cadets were confined to the steerage they looked at one another seriously.

" What do you suppose they'll do to us, Hal?"

" I'm sure I don't know," he replied; "if the charge was nothing more than overstaying our leave, I think we might get off easily."

" Well, that's all Mr. Crane mentioned."

" I know; but you may be sure that the Brazilian captain will make a formal complaint against us for helping Robert Lockwood to escape."

" But didn't Commander Brownson know we were going to help Captain Lockwood get his son?"

" Of course; I told him our whole plan. But then, you see, he had only to shut his eyes to our errand as long as the insurgents didn't catch us. Now the thing will be brought to his notice officially, and he'll be forced to take some action."

" All the same," said George, " he can't be very hard on us in the circumstances."

"But Mr. Crane seemed to be very angry with us for being aboard the *Aquidaban*."

"Well, we can explain that."

"All the same, I wish this thing hadn't happened."

"Me, too," said George, ungrammatically.

It was not more than two hours afterwards that Captain Lockwood arrived alongside the *Detroit*.

"I should like to see Cadets King and Briscomb," he said to the officer of the deck.

"Sorry, captain, but they're both under arrest."

"Arrest? What for?"

"Overstaying their leave and visiting the *Aquidaban*."

"Why, they couldn't help visiting her, and as for overstaying their leave, if they did, it was the Brazilian's doing, for he wouldn't put them aboard in time."

Mr. Harniss looked grave, and called for the orderly.

"Tell Commander Brownson that Captain Lockwood wishes to see him."

"Aye, aye, sir," said the marine, departing on his errand.

"But I haven't said anything of the sort," said the captain.

"You must tell the commander your story," said Mr. Harniss, "so as to set the boys right with him. It rests with him to release them without ordering a court-martial."

"I think I can make it all right," said the captain.

The orderly returned and took the merchant-skipper to the cabin.

"Good-afternoon, Captain Lockwood," said Commander Brownson. "What can I do for you?"

"You can't do anything for me, sir, but now that I'm here I want to thank you for the protection your ship gave my bark the other day."

"Oh, don't talk about that," said the commander. "You know that's what we're here for."

"Well, sir, I won't say anything more about it, if you don't want me to."

"I'm sure you didn't come to see me about that."

"No, sir; I came to see my young friends Cadets King and Briscomb, and I find they're under arrest. I know their offence was unavoidable, sir."

"How's that? Let me hear all about it."

Captain Lockwood rapidly narrated the events of the preceding night, laying especial stress on

Harold's coolness and courage. It speedily became apparent to Commander Brownson that the two young men had not intentionally violated the conditions of their leave, and the commander readily understood that the Brazilian captain had revenged himself by making them late. He sent for Harold and questioned him closely about the matter. The boy's frank and unhesitating answers convinced the commanding officer of his innocence. He dismissed the young cadet and sent for the executive officer.

"Mr. Crane," he said, "I am afraid we have made a slight mistake."

At the commander's request Captain Lockwood repeated his story to Mr. Crane, and the commander himself repeated the substance of his conversation with Harold.

"There is only one thing to do, sir," said Mr. Crane.

"What, sir?" asked the commander.

"The young men must be released from arrest at once, and it must be made known that their conduct has been satisfactory."

"You will attend to it at once. And now, Captain Lockwood, you may see your young friends."

"Well, sir, what I was going to say to them would have had to come to you in the end, so as long as I'm here I'd like to tell it to you myself."

" Go ahead, captain."

The merchant skipper proceeded to tell Commander Brownson the stories of his son and his nephew down to the preceding night.

" Now, sir," he said, " I wish first of all to save my son from being shot; I suppose that's natural enough, isn't it ?"

" My dear sir," said the commander, " you have my deepest sympathy."

" And, secondly, I want to get my nephew aboard my own bark, where my daughter and I can nurse him."

" I am afraid that cannot be accomplished. You see, he's an officer. Besides, what would you do for a physician ?"

" I am acquainted with the best doctor in Rio, and I could get him to come off every day."

Commander Brownson reflected for a few moments and then said :

" I know of only one way it may be done."

" How's that ?"

" By purchasing his discharge. The insurgents are hard pressed for money, and if they think he is going to be laid up long they might let him off for a small price."

"I'll go and see Admiral Da Gama at once," said the captain.

"I wouldn't go personally if I were you. He will not feel very cordial towards the captain of the *Alma*. Is there no one who is on good terms with him who would do you an errand?"

"No, not one — but wait! Yes, there is; there's Lieutenant Bennos, of the *Aquidaban*, my nephew's good friend."

"Just the man," said the commander.

"But about my son; can't I buy his discharge, too?"

"No, I fear not while he is under sentence of death. There is a big difference between a disabled officer and a condemned seaman."

"What's to be done, sir? My boy—my boy—he must be saved!"

"Captain Lockwood, I shall go at once and lay this case before Admiral Benham. His influence, I am sure, will be sufficient to get the sentence commuted. This rebellion cannot last much longer, and if we can save the boy's life, you'll be able to get him away to America when this silly war ends."

"God bless you, sir," said Captain Lockwood, in a voice shaken with emotion, as he shook the officer's hand warmly and left the cabin.

CHAPTER XXXII

A REBELLION IN COLLAPSE

COMMANDER BROWNSON did not altogether over-estimate the value of Admiral Benham's influence, yet the commander of the American fleet could get from the insurgent chief no further assurance than that Robert Lockwood's life would be spared for the present. Admiral Da Gama added that if he finally decided to execute the condemned boy he would give the American admiral due warning. It may well be understood that this condition of affairs put Captain Lockwood and his daughter into a fever of agonizing anxiety. Yet the American skipper was a man of great courage and energy, and he did not relax his efforts to save both his son and his nephew. The result of his talk with Lieutenant Bennos was that the latter placed the matter before his own commanding officer, without whose sanction he could not have applied to Admiral Da Gama. The captain of the *Aquida-ban* listened with patience, and, somewhat to the

15

surprise of Bennos, offered no objection to his proposition.

"It may as well be done now as later," he said, reflectively; "and the admiral will be very glad to get the money."

Accordingly Bennos visited the *Libertade* and laid the proposal of Captain Lockwood before the admiral.

"It is a matter of no great importance now," said Da Gama.

"Then I am to understand that you will sell the discharge of Frank Lockwood?"

"Yes, you may tell Captain Lockwood that I will accept his money and release the boy."

Bennos lost no time in conveying the joyful news to the American skipper, who promptly paid the sum agreed upon and received a written acknowledgment, together with a formal discharge of Frank. The next step was to secure the safe removal of the cadet from the *Aquidaban* to the *Alma*. This was by no means an easy task, for Frank was quite unable to leave his cot. It was necessary to wait a day or two until the weather was perfectly suitable. Then a cot was set up in the cabin of the *Alma*, and a stretcher which could be hoisted by a tackle was prepared. This stretcher was taken in the *Alma's* long-boat to the *Aquidaban*.

Frank was placed in it and carried on deck, and thence he was lowered into the boat. Arriving alongside the *Alma* he was hoisted aboard, and after the tackle was cast off he was carried below and put in the cot. He was greatly fatigued by the transfer, and for some hours he was inclined to be feverish. But finally youth and hope conquered, and he began to mend again.

"Uncle Hiram," he said, "I owe you a debt of gratitude which I can never repay."

"Don't think about that, Frank."

"I can't help it, Uncle Hiram. If I hadn't been foolish enough to enlist in this service—"

"I might never have found my boy, for it was you that put us on his track."

"But that did so little good."

"Nonsense, Frank. His life is spared for the present, and I haven't given up all hope of saving him by any means."

"Well, you've saved my life, sir."

"That's putting it pretty strong, Frank."

"The doctor on the *Aquidaban* said you would live," added Minnie.

"That may be so," said the boy; "but I'm sure I should have died if I'd had to stay in that service any longer."

The next day the two cadets on the *Detroit*

obtained permission to visit their friend. They sat by his cot for an hour and told him all that was going on in the American fleet.

" Watkins, Gleason, Briggs, and Brown have received orders to report for their final examination," said Hal.

" Yes, and they're going to New York by the steamer that sails to-morrow," said George.

Boom !

The thundering echo of a great gun rolled up the bay.

" What's that ?" asked the wounded boy.

" Oh, Frank !" exclaimed Minnie, running into the cabin, " the *Aquidaban* and the *Republica* are going out and the forts are firing upon them. I'm so glad you are not aboard."

" But Bob !" exclaimed Captain Lockwood, springing to his feet. " What 'll become of him ?"

" Let us go to Da Gama at once," cried Hal, hastening on deck, followed by the captain and George.

" A boat's comin' from the *San Francisco*, sir," said Mr. Ball.

In a few minutes a cadet from the flag-ship boarded the *Alma*. He had been sent to tell Captain Lockwood that Admiral Benham, hearing that Da Gama and Mello had quarrelled and that the *Aquidaban* and *Republica* were going south to engage in a vain attempt to carry on the rebellion on their own account, had sent a peremptory demand to Mello to know what was to be done with Robert Lockwood. The reply was that he had been surrendered to Admiral Da Gama. That commander had flatly refused to give any information further than to say that the boy was aboard one of his ships.

"I'll go and see him," said Captain Lockwood.

The cadets returned to their ships, and the American merchant captain visited the *Libertade*. But it was in vain, for he learned nothing. But Admiral Da Gama repeated his promise to send word to Admiral Benham as to any future treatment of Robert. Two days later George and Harold tumbled aboard the *Alma* with flushed faces.

"Old man," said Harold, "we've news for you."

"Yes," exclaimed George, "it's all over."

"What is all over?"

"The insurrection?"

"Has Da Gama surrendered?"

"No, but he has done something worse."

"What?"

"He has fled," said George.

"Yes," said Harold, "he has taken refuge on the Portuguese war-ships."

"And the government fleet is about to come up the bay."

At that moment the sound of heavy firing broke upon the air.

"Hurrah!" cried George. "The fun's begun."

"Oh!" exclaimed Frank, "I wish I could see it. May I, uncle? The doctor said I might sit up a little to-day."

"But I don't believe the excitement would be safe."

Minnie came and looked eagerly into her cousin's face.

"I am sure it would do him good, father," she said.

"Well, let's try it."

Harold and George brought a steamer-chair to the side of the cot, filled it with pillows and blankets, lifted Frank into it, and carried him on deck, where they stood beside him. The scene that met their eyes was inspiring. The batteries which President Peixoto had been planting on the hills had opened fire on the insurgent forts. Bursts of flame, followed by clouds of white smoke, were springing from the mountains as if they had all suddenly been transformed into volcanoes in active eruption. Crest echoed to

"THAT LOOKS LIKE BOB"

crest with the roar and rumble of artillery. From the insurgent forts arose clouds of dust as the shells fell and exploded within their walls. Out from behind Sugar Loaf, in a stately procession of single column, steamed the government fleet. The frowning *Nictheroy*, with her huge dynamite gun pointing like a titanic finger over her bow, led the way. Following in her wake were the *America* and the other ships, while the agile torpedo-boats spread out like skirmishers on the wings. Every vessel flew her bravest holiday bunting. The shores were lined with excited thousands, whose glad cheers rang loudly across the waters. But the insurgent ships and forts were as silent as graves. And when, a little later, President Peixoto's forces boarded the vessels and entered the forts, they found them utterly deserted. The rebellion in Rio Harbor had utterly collapsed.

Utterly deserted is not strictly true. On the poop-deck of the old *Tamandare* stood a single man. As the *Nictheroy* swept grandly past, this man hoisted the Brazilian flag to the peak and fired a shot from a musket. As a result his ship was boarded first, and a few minutes later the cutter from the *Nictheroy* shoved off again and headed towards the *Alma*.

" They're coming right this way," said Hal.

" And there's a man standing up in the boat and waving his hands," said Minnie.

" I may be weak and sick," said Frank, in an excited tone, " but I can see. That looks like Bob !"

CHAPTER XXXIII

AT SEA ONCE MORE

The boat came speeding up to the starboard side of the *Alma*. There was no longer any doubt that the excited young man was Robert Lockwood, and in a few seconds he was aboard the bark and in his father's arms. It was a deeply happy meeting for all concerned, and none of them were ashamed to be seen wiping the tears from their eyes.

"You are free and safe, my boy," said Captain Lockwood. "How did it all happen?"

"It's simple enough, father," replied Robert. "When the *Tamandare's* people received Admiral Da Gama's order to abandon ship and take refuge on the Portuguese man-of-war, there was a scene of wild confusion. There never was good discipline among the insurgents, and then there was none at all. I felt sure that they wouldn't stop to muster the crew, so I just dropped down into the fore-peak and kept quiet till they had all gone. After that I tried in a dozen ways to attract your attention, but of course you supposed that the ship's company was still aboard, and so you paid no attention. When I saw the *Nictheroy* coming up, I knew my chance was at hand. I succeeded in getting her to send a boat, and of course as more than half her officers are Americans, I had the good-luck to fall in with this gentleman, Lieutenant Hunt, and he brought me here."

Captain Lockwood warmly thanked the American, who now returned to his ship. Robert turned and shook hands once more with his cousin.

"Frank, old man," he said, "I don't know how to tell you of my grief at your being wounded. If it hadn't been for me, you'd never have come down here and enlisted."

"I can't say that, Bob, I can't say that. I was wild for active service, and I hadn't sense enough to see that in a foreign navy I ran the risk of being brought to quarters against the flag of my own country. It's been a terrible lesson to me. I'm afraid I should have come even if you hadn't been here, and now look at me. Out of the service, and stranded by the failure of this miserable rebellion."

"Cheer up, Frank," said Hal. "I know it's been hard, but I'm sure it was all for your good."

" Yes, I think that. I'm much changed, I believe."

" And so am I," said Robert. " Father, I ask your forgiveness for what I've done, and I promise you that from this time out I'll be guided by your wisdom."

" Then all this struggle hasn't been for nothing," said Captain Lockwood.

Two or three days later Harold and George again visited the *Alma*, bringing Peter with them.

" We have come to say good-bye, Frank," said Hal.

" You are going home?"

" Yes; the *Detroit* has been ordered to Norfolk. The whole fleet will be scattered in a little while," said George.

" God bless you, fellows! I wish I were going with you."

" Well, it won't be long before you follow," said Captain Lockwood. " My anchor has rusted in Rio mud long enough. I am going back to that precious wharf now and get my cargo."

" And then?" asked George.

" And then," replied Captain Lockwood, " I'm going to set sail for the land of civilization. The doctor says that Frank will improve at a twenty-

knot gait now, and in less than a week I hope
to be under way for New York."

" Hurrah for Central Park and the circus and
Coney Island!" cried George. "Oh, Frank, I
wish I were going with you."

" We may all meet sooner than we expect,"
said Frank. "You know we had no idea that
we should come together down here."

The two cadets shook hands with their friends,
and Captain Lockwood called Peter up out of
the boat.

"Shake hands, my lad," he said: "an honest
seaman's grip is what you will give and what you
will get."

" Thank ye, sir," said Peter, "an' a werry fair
wind an' a safe landfall to all of ye wherever
you're bound in this 'ere world, w'ich the same,
as my father used to say, it are a werry good
world, takin' it by an' large, allus perwidin' that
you steers a fair course."

When the *Detroit* passed out of the harbor the
Alma and the other American merchant ships
saluted her with every mark of respect. And
now Captain Lockwood hastened his preparations for departure. Robert busied himself
about the deck, and showed that he had already
learned a good deal of the duty of a seaman.
As for Frank, he picked up strength hand over

hand, and by the time the bark moved out to an anchorage again he was as well as he had ever been in his life. He was in the best of spirits, too. He was gentle and full of fun with his fair young cousin, whose affection for him was deepening every day. He was full of manly regard for his uncle and of honest gratitude towards him. His happiness manifested itself in many ways, but chiefly in buoyant activity. He sprang about the deck, lending a hand in the work of preparing the bark for sea, and his skill and readiness filled Captain Lockwood's heart with pride.

"A born sailor, that boy!" he exclaimed.

"Yes, sir," Mr. Ball responded; "both of 'em, and fit to command a ship."

"No, I'd hardly say that about Bob," said the captain. "and I don't care to have him so, either. But Frank certainly is."

It happened that two days before the bark was to sail Captain Lockwood's second mate left him to take a suddenly offered berth aboard a steamer. The captain was glad of it.

"What do you say, Frank?" he cried; "will you serve as my second mate on the voyage home?"

"Will I! Why, Uncle Hiram, I'll be only too glad."

"Then second mate of the *Alma* you are, my
boy," said the old skipper, striking his horny
palm into that of his nephew with a resounding
slap.

The morning chosen for the *Alma's* departure
was bright and beautiful, with a brisk southwesterly wind blowing. Captain Lockwood had instructed Frank as to the authority and responsi-
bilities of a second mate of a merchantman, and
the boy knew just what he had to do. Fold
after fold of the *Alma's* creamy canvas fell to its
length and was sheeted home, while Captain
Lockwood ordered the helm a-starboard, and the
anchor cleared the ground as the jib rose from
its boom. The *Alma* leaned gently over to
port, and began to glide away towards the narrow entrance of the harbor, beyond which the
rich blue of the South Atlantic spread a living
carpet for her tread.

"Get a pull on the fore and main braces!"
called the captain.

"Aye, aye, sir," answered Frank's fresh young
voice, as the boy led his men to their work.
"Now, my bullies, bowse her down."

"Born sailor, that boy," said Captain Lockwood, half aloud.

"And fit to command a ship," murmured Minnie,
echoing the favorite sentiment of the first mate.

The bark was on a taut bowline and turning the lucent blue into streaks of silver as she smoked out past Fort Santa Cruz.

"No one to fire on us going out," said the captain.

"And I am as free as a flying-fish," laughed Bob.

"I should think so," said Minnie. "They must be glad to get rid of us all."

"Poor wretches!" exclaimed her father, thinking of the insurgents, sick and wounded, penned up on the Portuguese war-ships.

"And I might have been one of them," said Frank.

The young second mate had the first dog-watch, and both Captain Lockwood and Mr. Ball studiously avoided the deck, and allowed the boy full command. There was little or nothing for him to do, except to heave the log and keep the record. In that work, however, he could have given instruction to both the older seamen, for he was an expert navigator. Minnie was on hand to watch him at his duties, and she was of the opinion that he was the finest young officer she had ever seen.

"The lad 'll have the first watch," said Mr. Ball.

"Yes," said the captain, "and I shouldn't be

surprised if he had a chance to show what he knows. These southwesterly winds often freshen at night in these latitudes."

As for Frank, he had already detected signs of growing strength in the breeze, but the *Alma* was a great sail-carrier, and it did not take him long to find it out. Nearly through the first dog-watch he let her boil through it with her royals on, but at the last moment he decided that though she could carry them she would do as well without them. So he sung out:

"Aloft to furl royals! Man the royal clew-lines, flying-jib downhaul! Haul taut! In royals, down flying-jib! Furl the royals! Stow the flying-jib!"

"Listen to him," said Captain Lockwood, in the cabin. "He's doing it in man-o'-war style."

"Bless you, sir, he'll soon get over that. You see, he knows how to do it, anyhow."

The sailors by this time knew that their young second mate was a thorough seaman, and they obeyed him with a will. When Frank went on deck again for the first watch he found that the wind was gaining in power all the time, and that Mr. Ball had furled the top-gallants. An hour later the boy decided that the courses ought to be taken in, so he sent word to the captain, who at once came on deck and gave the necessary orders. It now became Frank's duty to go aloft and take the bunt of the main-sail. If he had shown any lack of strength or skill it would have been no great disgrace, for second mates are not always the best sailors. But the seamen who lay out on the main-yard with Frank found that the Annapolis training was sound. The boy knew his business, and had plenty of strength. The sail was taken in with neatness and despatch.

"Well done, Frank!" shouted the captain, when the boy regained the deck.

"Oh, Uncle Hiram," he said, "I feel as if I could haul up the main-topsail reef-tackle of an old-time line-of-battle ship all by myself."

"You do?"

"Yes, sir. I am no longer in the service of a foreign power. I've got an American keel under me, and I'm bound for an American port."

"I'm glad you're so happy, my boy."

"Happy! Bless you, Uncle Hiram, I'm overjoyed. I feel that I am going back to New York to begin life over again; to take it up where I made the false start, and to try to do better. I've learned my lesson, sir, and I'll not forget it. Go it, old bark! You're making a dozen knots
16

an hour, and taking one fellow away from the scene of his greatest folly."

"Two, Frank," said Robert, taking his cousin's hand.

CHAPTER XXXIV

A HAPPY REUNION

A YEAR had passed since the events related in the opening chapter of this story. The brave American fleet which had assembled in the harbor of Rio de Janeiro to protect the interests of United States citizens had scattered far and wide. The *San Francisco* had gone to Nicaragua, where internal dissensions placed Americans in jeopardy, and she had in a short time been followed by the armored cruiser *New York*. The *Detroit* had gone back to the navy-yard at Norfolk, whence she had set forth with our two young friends on their first cruise in the active service of the flag, and the good little ship was undergoing needed repairs. The *Alma* had reached New York after a quick passage, discharged her cargo, and made a short voyage to Halifax and back. Mr. Ball had resigned his post for a comfortable berth ashore, and Frank had been promoted to the position of first mate. He had learned to like the merchant service, and, seeing no other vocation open to him at the time, had

gratefully accepted the appointment from his
uncle. Robert, steadied by his own unhappy experience, had yielded to his father's wish that he
should remain ashore, and was now a clerk in the
captain's office, with a fine prospect of succeed-
ing to his father's business.

The bark was lying at a wharf on the East
River front, preparing for a new voyage to South
American ports, with Rio de Janeiro as her final
destination. Frank was as busy as a bee superintending the preparations. Captain Lockwood
was aboard the vessel, but he contented himself
with sitting in the cabin or in a big chair under
an awning spread over the quarter-deck, for an
old enemy, rheumatism, the result of many years
of exposure to wind and rain, had possession of
him. Minnie had come down from the house,
and it had been decided that they should all
dine aboard the bark. Suddenly the clatter of
rapidly approaching footsteps was heard, and a
voice sang out from the wharf:

" Aboard the *Alma !*"

Frank turned his head, and to his great surprise and joy saw Harold King, George Briscomb, and Peter Morris standing opposite the
vessel waving their hats. The cadets were in
civilian clothing, but every movement betokened
their familiarity with salt water.

"Hello, fellows!" shouted Frank. "Come aboard!"

The boys sprang up the gang-plank and threw their arms around Frank.

"God bless you, old man!" said Harold. "How well you look!"

"I should say so," said George. "You don't look like the ghost we left in Rio Harbor."

"Beggin' your pardon, sir," said Peter, "but you looks like you owned most o' the East River an' could borrow the North without givin' no security."

"Where's the captain?" asked Hal.

"And your pretty cousin?" added George.

"They're both in the cabin."

"Let's give them a surprise, Hal," said George.

The next minute the two boys tumbled into the cabin like two young bears.

"How are you, captain?" cried George, seizing the mariner's big hand and shaking it enthusiastically.

"Avast there, boy; I've got the rheumatics!" cried the seaman, laughing in spite of the twinges.

"And how's the sailor girl?" demanded George.

"Oh, we're all well and happy," said Minnie, flushed with excitement and pleasure at the meeting.

"Did you see Frank?" asked the captain.

" Yes, we certainly did," answered Hal.

" And did you notice what he was up to ?"

" Seemed to me to be a sort of rear-admiral of the whole business," said George.

" He's my first mate," said the captain, proudly.

" You don't mean it !" exclaimed Hal, with a delighted face.

" Yes, and a better one I never had," declared the captain, emphatically.

" That's fine news," said the cadet.

" And now I want you boys to stay and have dinner with us," said the captain.

" Aboard the *Alma ?*"

" Yes."

" Well, sir, there's nothing in the world could give us greater pleasure at this minute," exclaimed Hal.

" Minnie, girl, you go and tell Kibo that we're going to have a dinner-party, and we want the best he can set out, because it's the chief mate's birthday."

" Frank's birthday ?" cried the young men.

" Yes, he's twenty-one to-day, and it's going to be a red-letter day."

" Let's go and congratulate him," said George.

The two boys bounded out on deck and shook Frank's hand till he was sore.

"We wish you many happy returns of the day, old man."

"Thank you, fellows. I'd like it to come pretty often if it would bring you with it."

Then the two young men ran back to the cabin and shook hands with the captain, and congratulated him on having such a good fellow as Frank for a nephew.

"He is a good boy and a fine seaman, and that unhappy experience of his in the Brazilian insurgent navy has steadied and made a man of him."

An hour passed and Kibo, the cook, had the dinner ready. Robert had been sent for and was heartily greeted by the cadets. In some mysterious way, which could be attributed only to Minnie, some pretty flowers appeared on the table, and the cabin was filled with the perfume of summer and youth. Seated at the head of his generous board, Captain Lockwood had a beneficent smile.

"Children," he said, "I'm free to say this is one of the brightest days I've known in a reasonably prosperous life. I'm about to propose the health of my dear nephew."

"Hear, hear!" shouted Peter, who had not been left out of the happy gathering.

"What I desire to do," continued the captain,

" is to have my two boys—for Frank's as good
as a son to me—"

" And a brother to me," said Bob.

" Don't interrupt," said the captain. " I want
these two boys to carry on my business after
I'm a sheer hulk. So, Bob, I'd like to know if
you're willing to have me give Frank an interest
in the business ?"

" Yes, and a big one, too," said Bob, heartily.

" No, no ; share and share alike. From this
day you each have half."

" Oh, Uncle Hiram !" exclaimed Frank.

" Hear, hear !" shouted Peter, again.

" Avast there, my hearty," said the captain.
laughing. " I'm getting along in years, and I've
got rheumatism, and I guess I'd better stay
ashore after this. So I want you all to stand
up and give three cheers for the youngest merchant skipper in America, Captain Frank Lockwood, of the bark *Alma*."

" Hurrah ! hurrah ! hurrah !" shouted the two
boys.

For a few seconds Frank was pale and silent.
Then he said :

" Uncle Hiram, do you put me in command of
this bark ?"

" Yes, and you're the only member of her company that didn't know it till this minute."

"'RUN IT UP,' SAID FRANK."

" Let us go on deck," said Frank, gravely.

They passed out of the cabin, and the crew, knowing what had happened, gave Frank a cheer. He lifted his cap, and said :

" Quartermaster, get the ensign and bend it on the halyards."

The order was obeyed.

" Run it up," said Frank, taking off his cap and facing aft, while the others imitated him.

When the flag reached the peak of the spanker-gaff he put on his cap, turned, and wrung his uncle's hand.

" Uncle Hiram," he said, " I'll do my best to deserve the trust you have reposed in me. Every morning at eight bells that flag will go up, and every evening at sunset it will come down, and as I shall never again be unfaithful to it, so I shall never be unfaithful to you."

He turned to the two cadets and grasped their hands.

" Fellows, you've been real friends. Hal, if I'd been as cool and steady as you I'd never have turned my back on the flag."

" But you've had your punishment, old man, and now the future is bright before you."

" Bob," said Frank, turning and clasping his cousin's hand, " you and I have got a good deal more than we deserve, but we'll try to make your father feel that he's done wisely, won't we?"

"That we will," replied Bob.

And then Minnie, with her eyes full of tears, ran up and kissed both of them.

"Jee-whiz!" exclaimed Peter; "as my mother used to say w'en she were eatin' huckleberry pie, 'This 'ere's good 'nuff fur me.'"

THE END

www.ingramcontent.com/pod-product-compliance
Lightning Source LLC
Chambersburg PA
CBHW020859020726
47497CB00005B/1486